Race

from the Finish

D. T. Dignan

abbott press®
A DIVISION OF WRITER'S DIGEST

Race from the Finish

Cover image by Mary DuPrie Studios. Photo shot at
Waterford Hills Road Racing, Michigan.

Certain characters in this work are historical figures, and certain
events portrayed did take place. However, this is a work of fiction.
All of the other characters, names, and events as well as all places,
incidents, organizations, and dialogue in this novel are either the
products of the author's imagination or are used fictitiously.

Abbott Press books may be ordered through booksellers or by contacting:

Abbott Press
1663 Liberty Drive
Bloomington, IN 47403
www.abbottpress.com
Phone: 1-866-697-5310

ISBN: 978-1-4582-0565-0 (sc)
ISBN: 978-1-4582-0564-3 (e)

Library of Congress Control Number: 2012914473

Printed in the United States of America

Abbott Press rev. date: 09/05/2012

To Daddy Max.

A slight turn of the wheel and our course is forever altered.

Acknowledgments

WHILE A WORK OF fiction, I have invested much care and research to render the story as historically accurate as possible.

Thanks are due to racing expert Rob Mathiesen, who shared his expertise on topics including racing form, what goes through the driver's mind during a race, and potential mechanical failures that could befall a 1940 Ford sport coupe on a dirt track.

I also owe much appreciation to Jeff Iula of the All-American Soap Box Derby, for responding to my inquiry several years ago when the novel was first under way. He kindly provided information and actual photos of races from the 1940s. Those photos sparked life into the telling of the scene and made the section a joy to write.

Prologue

JUST THIS MORNING, I said to myself, "Thaddeus, why are you having that dream again?" It must be poor Mr. Powers in room 210 that's on my mind. It's a shame about Mr. Powers. The poor soul is lying there, and not one person has come to visit. Every night he lies in the dark and calls out for someone to help him, his voice so faint it barely makes it into the hallway:

"Help. Someone, help me."

God knows I wish I could. The nurses do a good job keeping him comfortable, but he still carries on until they ignore him. I say a prayer, when he starts in, that the good Lord will take care of him in the next life better than He has in this one.

Working the afternoon shift doesn't bother me. I've been at it for thirty years and seen a lot of things you wouldn't want to talk about: human frailty and sickness and stench, people at their worst. We die slow or we die fast, but some people seem in a rush to get life over with. They're brought here all bloody and broken up, or poisoned with alcohol and drugs, so we can try to fix 'em up and send 'em on their way. Most poor souls have just tried to do the best they could and ended up with some malady or another. The docs figure out what's ailing them and do what they can.

Thank God, I'm just a tech and not one of those docs tryin' to save people's lives. Oh, the folks that get better are all right. It's the other ones, alone in their dark rooms hooked up to artificial life, looking at you with pleading eyes waiting for the end, the ones that the docs can't to nothing for. I'm pretty good at keeping a distance, but now and again I see some of those faces in my sleep. Just the other day, I had that dream again, the same dream that troubles me at least twice a year, shaking me awake hot and sweaty with the sheets sticking like fly paper.

I'm standing next to the patient's bed and it's dark except for one little white light over the bed. He's breathing heavily and looking scared while I pull on gloves and prepare the stretcher to take him to the mortuary. This would never happen in real life, him still being alive and all, but dreams turn everything around. He stops breathing, so I lift him onto the gurney and cover him with a white sheet, cover his face with his empty eyes staring at nothing. It's always the same face: stern but silent and not like any other I remember. Trouble is I can't seem to remember whose face it is once I wake up.

Anyway, I'm rolling the gurney down a long hallway toward the mortuary, and damn if the tears aren't rolling down my face like a baby. The hall is dark and lonely except for a few dim overhead lights reflecting off the gray linoleum floor. It's so empty; the squeak of my rubber soles echoes off the walls. That's usually when I wake up with that sick, helpless sensation in the pit of my gut.

Word around the hospital is that John Powers used to be quite the stock-car driver in his day—back in the '50s and into the '80s. I don't follow racing myself, but I know it takes a strong man to handle a car at those speeds. You'd never know it by the looks of him. I overheard the night nurse say he has a son arriving from Chicago in two days. Two days. It seems nowadays a body could get to Pittsburgh from Chicago faster than two days. It will be a miracle if he makes it in time to see his father still alive. My own two boys have never been particularly affectionate, but if it were me lying in there, by God they'd be here in a New York minute. Of course, I don't know why it should concern me; the man means nothing to me. He's just another stranger preparing to leave with nothing—just as he entered this world. His own family won't come see him, poor devil. I suppose there's a reason. There is always a reason.

Chapter One

"Now Johnny, Johnny, listen to me. Don't be looking around. Just focus straight ahead on the bottom of the hill ..."

"I *know*, Dad. I know."

Johnny climbed in his shiny red Soap Box Derby racer with the number 23 stenciled on each side in white paint and gripped the metal steering wheel in his small hands. His palms molded to the shape of the smooth metal, the wheel hot from the August sun.

Johnny Powers knew a thing or two about derby racing. Winning local derby heats and finally the Pittsburgh championship, he knew this was his big chance at glory. City champions could only race once at Derby Downs. He had worked hard to participate. Taking up the hobby took weeks of begging, of diligently completing his chores, until his mother allowed him to work at Pop's Garage and Filling Station on Tuesdays and Thursdays. Business had been steady since the war stopped production of new automobiles, and Pop often worked into the evening. Biking the four blocks from school, he fetched tools for the mechanics, emptied garbage bins, stocked supplies, and cleaned windshields until suppertime. At fifty cents a week, it seemed forever until Johnny had saved the six dollars to buy the wheels and axles that B. F. Goodrich Co. manufactured specifically for participants.

"You just do like I say and you'll come out fine. This track is faster than home." Patrick Powers squeezed the shoulder of his eleven-year-old son. "I'll see you when it's over."

Johnny nodded and peered ahead at the 975 feet and three lanes of paved track glistening black in the sun. Seated in the Soap Box Derby racer he had crafted himself, he felt confident yet a bit nervous about racing in the All-American. It was his first chance since the war had halted the event just as he reached qualifying age.

"Okay, Dad." Johnny mustered a smile as his father trotted off toward the sidelines.

Sponsored by the *Pittsburgh Post-Gazette*, Johnny and his father had taken the trip to Akron, Ohio with the racer tied down in the back of Dad's dusty, black pickup. They arrived at Derby Downs three days before the event and participated in some of the activities held for racers and their families. Firestone Tire & Rubber Company sponsored entertainment, and Johnny had met the local radio personality and more than one Hollywood celebrity. He felt like a star in his own right. A photo of Johnny standing next to his racer after the

Pittsburgh championship, a broad white smile on his tanned face, had made the front page of the *Gazette*. Everyone in town knew of his accomplishment. His picture graced the grocer's display window next to the ad for the daily specials, and Ed's barbershop promised a year of free haircuts to the boy who had been a loyal patron since the age of two. The height of celebrity status occurred in Akron on race day. Johnny, dressed in white pants and a silk jacket, proudly carried in the pre-race parade a white flag sporting the Soap Box Derby logo and the word "Pittsburgh" boldly printed in clean black. The armed forces had even shown up to start the affair. A flatbed truck eased down the track carrying Marines reenacting the raising of the American flag at the summit of Mount Suribachi during the battle of Iwo Jima.

Along with the prestige of winning in front of over fifty thousand fans, the winner of the All-American would receive a college scholarship, a cash prize, a trophy, and an airplane trip for his family to New York City from Firestone Company. Johnny gripped the steering wheel harder as he thought about how proud his father would be when they all got to fly in an airplane for the first time, all because of him. Because of what he had done on his own, completely alone, with only a few bits of advice from Pop while he built the racer in the back corner of the garage.

She had become his first love. Never before in his young life had Johnny cared so much about something. Thoughts of the emerging racer and the glory they would share together poked through at all times of the day. The racer silently waited for him to arrive after school and on Saturday afternoons for each step of the process to be completed. He would have spent Sundays with her if Pop hadn't closed the garage. Besides,

Momma would have no part of him spending the Lord's day working on a racecar. Momma got religion after Susan was born. Johnny was only six when Susan came home from the hospital, yet he could tell that something was different about his little sister. Momma looked at her with love and sadness mingled in her eyes, neighbors whispered the strange word "mongoloid" after seeing the baby (if Momma was out of earshot), and Susan's face had an almond-eyed look.

With the smell of motor oil and rubber blended with the pot roast or ham sandwich Momma packed for his dinner, Johnny had worked in silence, visualizing how the All-American Soap Box Derby track would look. He imagined the smell of hot pavement baking in the summer sun and the cheer of spectators as he breezed past the finish line in first place.

"Don't you think it's 'bout time you got home?" Pop would emerge from under the hood of a Buick or Hudson, smearing grease from his hands onto a large, red kerchief that he stored in the front pocket of his overalls. A stout man of about fifty-five, with strong features softened by friendly eyes, Pop was the closest thing to a grandpa Johnny knew. Pop had known Johnny's family for many years. Dad told him Pop had been his foreman at the steel mill when he was just starting out, before he even met Momma. Only Dad knew Pop's Christian name; to everyone else, he was just Pop. Many a holiday and Sunday afternoon, Momma would fret that Pop had no wife to cook for him. It was no trouble to put an extra potato and a few carrots in the soup. Dad would get on the phone, and soon Pop was rapping at the front door. Since he raved so over Momma's cooking, it was no wonder she liked having him around.

"In a minute," Johnny often replied as he appeared next to Pop. The boy watched Pop's thick hands, darkened from dirty oil and scarred from his trade, working magic to repair sick engines, sluggish transmissions, and worn body parts. No doctor of medicine could have inspired as much awe as Johnny felt toward Pop. He was a savior in soiled overalls and a flannel shirt, but Johnny loved him most for his quiet and safe presence. If Pop ever removed the blue-and-white-striped conductor's hat from his head, Johnny felt certain a halo would emerge.

The evening wasn't complete until the young protégé had riddled his teacher with questions. "What's that thermometer thing with the colored balls?" "Why does such a little crack in the distributor cap cause so much trouble?" "How much horsepower does an engine have?" "Why doesn't oil freeze in the winter?"

One evening in particular, Pop had just finished installing new tires on a Desoto and lifted the hood to adjust the carburetor air intake. "Why don't you make yourself useful and start 'er up for me?"

Johnny's eyes grew large. He had never sat behind the wheel of a car, let alone started the engine. "Really? You bet!"

He raced around to the driver's side and then caught himself, slowing, gingerly opening the heavy door, admiring the smooth, banana-meat-yellow finish. As he slid inside, soft caramel leather enveloped him, the odor of tobacco and leather lingering in his nostrils. He reached his thin arms up to the steering wheel and pulled himself forward, perching on the seat's edge to allow the tip of his shoe to reach the gas pedal. *Let's see; yes, it is in park.* The silver key enticed him to touch, to realize power he had never experienced at the turn of his fingers. He took the key in his fingers and licked his lips with the anticipation of it. *Better pump the gas a few times to make sure. Turn slowly, one click, step on the gas, then all the way.* The engine roared to life, racing from too much gas and filling the garage with a deafening growl.

Shocked, Johnny fell back in the seat and released his foot from the pedal.

"Whoa, Powerhouse!" Pop yelled. "Save that for the races."

Johnny sheepishly emerged from the Desoto while Pop, sporting a jovial smirk, entered the car and kicked the gas pedal. The engine settled to an even rumble.

"What did you call me just then?" Johnny asked as Pop walked around to reach under the hood."

"Powerhouse? Oh, it was just a joke."

"No, I like it. Really. It has my name in it. You can call me that anytime you want."

"Well then, Powerhouse," Pop said as he extended a large hand to the boy at his side, "nice to meet you."

From that day on, Pop no longer referred to his young friend as Johnny.

Satisfied with his day's work, Johnny would pedal his rickety red Schwinn toward home under a blanket of twilight, his muscles sore from sanding wood to a smooth finish. Momma always met him at the back door, a bowl of warm milk over bread sprinkled with sugar waiting on the kitchen table to "help the sandman come." Susan was already asleep by then. Dad usually delayed until his radio show was interrupted with a sponsor break before asking, "How'd it go today, son?"

Patrick Powers was a man of simple tastes—quiet in spirit and as dedicated to the steel mill as he was to his family. He let his only son hold the reins on his racecar project, only interjecting his opinion when Johnny asked for it, or driving him to the hardware store to get supplies.

The trip to the hardware store was a special event, Johnny pouring over the color samples as a librarian might finger manuscripts. Black was too official, white was boring, and yellow was too garish. He settled on a bright red that reminded him of his Radio Flyer wagon and how his used Schwinn must have looked when it was new. Once he had selected the paint, all that he needed to do was to pick the number. He chose 23 for his birth date of October 23, 1934. Finally, she emerged as a glorious red racer, her elongated egg shape shining in the sun as Johnny's father rolled her up two wooden planks into his truck bed.

Number 23 was smooth and easy to handle. Patrick Powers transported her to the local hill on Saturdays after dinner so Johnny could get acquainted with the downhill track. Johnny felt confident when race day arrived in May. He had won the first heat by a full car length and continued to inch past each contestant to take the championship. He had expected nothing less.

Now perched at the top of derby hill, Johnny snapped to the present amid shouts of encouragement erupting from the sidelines. Hearing his father's voice, Johnny turned to scan the multitude of faces.

"Hey, Johnny, win it for Pittsburgh!"

Overhead, the Goodyear blimp crawled along a cloudless sky.

"You're up, son," a white-clad attendant said as he grabbed the rim of the racer and rolled it toward the starting point. A wood panel stood erect and kissed the nose of the racer, holding it in place. This was his first heat. If Johnny qualified, he would go on to compete until someone won the championship. He was positioned in the far right lane—lane three—and from there he spied his competition in the two adjacent lanes. The kid in the center lane was all business. His blue racer, his face, and his hands were smeared with a thin layer of black graphite. His appearance drew a long stare from the young boy in the farthest lane.

"Say! Al Jolson's shown up for the race!" a male voice boomed from behind the spectator fence.

The fence was a temporary, rickety, and thin-planked affair only three feet high. Behind it stood hundreds upon hundreds of people extending from just a few yards behind the track and into the trees beyond. Small boys pressed against the fence, wishing for a chance to be in a car of their own, lank arms hanging over the edge in an effort to be closer to the activity on the other side. Farther down the track, at the finish line, stood grandstands packed with noisy spectators. Johnny looked down toward the stands where thousands of people waited and looked at the slender kid from Pittsburgh seated in a maraschino-cherry-red racer. The voices became one voice, ebbing and swelling in his ears like the waves of an angry sea. He focused on the reporters' stand perched over the finish line. Topped with loudspeakers, the stand was dotted with newsmen and photographers clad in white shirts and dark ties. A line of sixteen American flags hung loosely in the summer heat.

Panic jumped in his chest and slowly settled into his stomach. What if the racer didn't perform well or he should make a costly steering mistake? Why did he have to race against the aerodynamic wonder in the next lane? He closed his eyes to shut off the valve of negative commentary that threatened to drown his glory. His heart beat fast with the realization that thousands were waiting for him to perform, to win, to show them how it could be done. He was sitting in a racer and they were not.

The reality of it grabbed him by the shoulders and shook him to attention in the few seconds it took to position the racer at the starting line. A slight grin eased over his face as he shimmied down into the seat and leaned forward, his eyes sandwiched between his helmet and the top of the racer. The panic waned, replaced with anticipation that oozed from the crowed and spread over him like warm butter on toast.

"Ready!" a male voice shouted from behind, making Johnny jump in his seat. He focused on the ribbon of pavement that was wide near his car and narrowed to a slim strip of licorice at its base.

"Easy," he whispered to himself. "This is easy."

"Three, two, one!" All at once, the wooden panel fell to the ground with a slap and the racers began rolling down the hill.

They picked up speed once the crest was behind them. Johnny dared not look away from the dashed white line marking the center of his lane, yet his peripheral vision told him he was clearly in front. His racer smoothed down the hill, faster still, until the wind gliding over the hood caused his eyes to sting with tears; he had forgotten to lower his goggles, which were still perched on his helmet.

He was doing well! The cheers grew louder as the three boys passed the midway point. Almost there! He had it for sure!

Or did he?

He had to be certain. Quickly, Johnny jerked his head to the left to see where his opponents stood. As he did, the center stripe slid to the right. He turned the steering wheel ever so slightly to get back to center but overcompensated and had to turn back again to straighten out. Finally at center point, he saw a dark spot enter the far corner of his left eye. He dared not turn to look. The spot grew larger until Johnny could make out the front of the graphite kid's racer inching ahead. Distracted, Johnny crouched even lower, willing speed into every fiber of his body.

Only twenty yards to go. Come on!

He urged number 23 to go faster, yet the blue racer in the next lane slowly came closer, closer into view, until Johnny could almost make out the front wheels.

The red racer from Pittsburgh did not win the first heat. Johnny's heart sank to his shoes as the finish line slipped under his wheels within a second behind the blue racer.

It was over.

He climbed from the racer, his legs shaking from the adrenaline pumping through his body, removed his leather helmet, and glanced toward the other racers. Both boys were flush with the excitement of the race, even the kid who finished last.

Johnny could only stew over not placing first. He had invested everything into this day, and it sped by him in less than thirty seconds. He looked at his red racer, feeling apologetic. She was a great racer; he had let her down by not staying focused.

An attendant, clad in white from his safari sun hat to his shoes, guided the young racer and his car off the track. Johnny peered up derby hill and made a crucial decision. From that point on, he would accept nothing short of winning.

Suddenly, Johnny remembered to scan the crowd for his father. Had he seen him look away, ever so briefly, during the race? He looked intently at the multitude but could not find his father among them. There was some comfort knowing his father would be upbeat about the day, regardless of the result. Patrick Powers was not the accusatory type. It was Johnny's own gnawing sense of disappointment and failure that would accompany him on the long ride home.

Chapter Two

JOHN HUSHED THE ALARM to avoid waking his parents and groggily threw his gangly teenage legs over the side of the bed. Just 4:30 on a Sunday morning: his parents would not rouse until at least 7:30 for the customary pancakes and coffee before church at 9:00. That should give him plenty of time, if he hustled.

He threw on a shirt and slacks and pushed his feet into loafers by the soft light of his bedside lamp. No time to shower or brush his teeth, not even to splash cold water on his face. He carefully thumbed the bills in his wallet and slid it into his pocket, along with a comb and keys. With pained slowness, he turned the knob and pulled open the bedroom door. From down the hall, snoring rose and fell. Good. Dad was sound asleep.

John cautiously shut the bedroom door so his parents would not notice his empty, unmade bed upon heading downstairs. Creeping into the hallway and down the stairs, careful to avoid the third and fifth steps and risk being exposed by their creaking, he gingerly opened the front door.

It clicked closed behind him.

Once outside in the chill March air, he sprinted, cursing his failure to grab a coat and hat. Piles of hardened snow festooned the edges of each driveway he passed. The run did little to warm him but made his heart race all the more.

After several blocks, he arrived at Pop's Garage. The shop rested dark, still, somber. His cold fingers fumbled in his pocket for the key that gained entry to the front office and waiting area. Making his way to the door leading to the garage, he felt a rush of adrenaline that made his hand shake on the doorknob.

"It's okay," he assured himself. "Pop will understand when I explain everything. I hope."

John opened the first bay door and snatched the set of keys from their peg on the garage wall. He used one to unlock the tow truck parked there and turned over the engine. The gas gauge read less than a quarter tank. *Better be sure.* He pulled out to the sole pump on the lot and added five gallons, closed the bay door, and then jumped into the truck.

The tow rattled and clanked with each bump as he sped over the highway east toward the outskirts of town. The road was dark and solitary at this hour, leaving John alone with his thoughts.

One thing pervaded them: the prize at the end of his trek.

Forty miles later, he turned onto the dirt road leading to the junkyard and pulled up to the gate. A single floodlight beamed from a tall pole at the entrance. John parked the truck and stepped up to the gate. There was no sound, no one around. What if the owner had forgotten to meet him here as planned? His heart began to sink. He rested his hands on the cold steel gate and watched his breath crystallize.

A low growl emanated from the darkness beyond. John strained to see a dark shape move where a thin strip of earth separated piles of metal. The shape grew larger and bounded toward the gate with panting breath. John instinctively released his grip on the gate as the sleek form of a Doberman took shape. The dog bared his teeth and then let loose a rampage of snarls and barks that made John jump back and trip over the tow truck's bumper.

"It's all right, boy. Don't blow a gasket," came a thin male voice from the darkness.

John righted himself and recognized the yard owner slowly approaching. A rumpled man in faded jeans and oil-stained coat, he opened the gate just enough to squeeze in and chain the Doberman, now calmer but still on the alert.

Head down, he walked into the yard as John followed behind. "Is this the only time of day you could get here?" the man whined. "Not only is it my day off, but I had to git up early and leave the missus in a tizzy about workin' on Sunday."

"I'm sorry," John responded. "This was the only time I could get the truck."

"Huh," the man grunted as he glanced back at the tow truck cleanly painted with "Pop's Garage: the best service, the best price." He said, "You know how to use that thing?"

"Yeah, sure." John had never actually towed anything, but he had watched Pop a few times. How hard could it be?

"Good, 'cause I'm not stickin' 'round long once you're through. Was out late last night and I'm dog tired."

The man shuffled past rusted shells of automobiles and piles of misshapen metal that at one time had made up the innards of some mechanical wonders. John followed in silence, too intense to notice the navy-blue sky slowly morph to soft turquoise or the morning's first bird calls.

There she sat: white paint dull from oxidization, rounded fenders lined with rust, cracked tires, and sun-faded black interior. The hood slimmed to a softly curved point flanked by rounded fender hips housing the yellowed headlights; she looked like the posterior side of a reposing cat. She was the most beautiful thing John had ever laid eyes on. No engine, spotted with rust, the '40 Ford coupe's tall grill seemed to smile at the sight of him.

"Twenty-five dollars, right?" John flipped open his wallet.

"That's what I told ya t'other day."

John handed the bills over.

"Hope you don't need a receipt," the man said. "I left my receipt book in the office."

"No, that's fine. It's fine. I'll just hook her up and be on my way."

"Well then," the dealer said as he extended a hand which John shook vigorously, "good luck to ya. I'll be in the office for a bit. Honk on your way out so I know to lock the gate."

The rumpled man shuffled off, head down, toward the entrance.

John rested his hand on the coupe's round fender. She was a sorry sight from exposure and neglect, nothing a lot of work wouldn't fix. She didn't need to look pretty, just run fast. For what he needed, she was perfect. He would drop in a flathead V-8, replace the tires, clean up the rust, and create the most incredible racecar in the Pittsburgh circuit.

John ran through the junkyard under a brightening sky and started the tow truck. He slowly wheeled his way through the yard and backed as close as he could to the Ford. Releasing the tow hook, he slid under the Ford, found a hole in the frame's underside, and slid the hook up and through. The action knocked a bit of rust loose and it fell on his face. He brushed it aside and scurried to open the door, released the hand brake, and slid the shift lever into neutral. He had to get back to the garage and then home before he was missed.

The tow's engine rumbled as he popped back into the cab. A separate key started the tow's hydraulic lift. Slowly, slowly the chain wound. The Ford's front end lifted off the ground. *Come on!* John felt the urgency to get on the road. No need to lift too high—a few feet should do. John switched off the hydraulic and cautiously pulled his prize behind him through the junkyard. He honked twice on his exit as the yard keeper, looking a bit more awake, waved him off and closed the gate.

"Yaaaa Hooo!" John whooped as he turned off the dusty yard lot onto the main road.

The road was absent of other cars at this hour. Pavement sliding under the wheels, the sound of the truck's engine, and the occasional clank of the chain over dips or bumps in the pavement accompanied John on his trip back toward town.

He glanced at his watch—ten past six. What if Momma woke early like she was prone to do? He couldn't let her see him enter the house. She couldn't know about the coupe just yet. He had to wait until the perfect moment to tell his parents about the Ford and his plans to race by midsummer. They would think it was a waste of time and money. Dad probably wouldn't mind so much, but Momma would never understand. She might make him stop. Perhaps if he had already worked on the car, had invested time and money before she found out, she would be less inclined to put a stop to his plans. Yes, the later they knew about it the better.

Of course, Pop would find out tomorrow when he saw a used-up white Ford parked in the back of the garage. He would be angry about John taking the tow without telling him first, but then he would simmer down. Pop wasn't like other adults. Wasn't as stiff and set in his ways. John knew he could rely on Pop's support. Now he began to worry about the excuse he would give Momma if she caught him coming back in the house when he was supposed to be in bed.

He was hungry and went to the diner. No, the diner didn't open until 11:00, and the rest of town all but shut down on Sundays. He decided to give the tow more gas and hasten his arrival at the garage. Glancing in the rear-view mirror, he could just see the windshield and glaring white top of his new baby. He smiled and relaxed in his seat. Everything was going to be great.

Careening down the two-lane highway, John thought about working on the Ford to get her race-ready. Pop could order whatever he needed at cost from his distributors. What parts weren't available could be tooled.

Mesmerized by the engine's constant vibration and miles of rolling country, John let himself slip into sweet meditation. The tow truck strained up a steep hill and John floored the pedal to keep up speed, just at the crest where it always seemed hardest, then let up as the truck slipped over the top. Just past the top, into the downhill, the truck gave a slight shimmy that rattled the tow even louder. *Probably the trans.* He wondered if the coupe would need a new transmission. If they could not find the right engine to snug up to the existing tranny, he would be replacing it. Thank God, Pop would let him work extra hours to pay for what he needed.

The downhill came fast, and John tapped the brake to ease the descent. He'd have to check the Ford's brakes for rust though the yard owner said she had only been there a few months. The previous owner destroyed the engine—apparently some people didn't know that oil has to be changed more than once a decade. She was in good hands now.

John's reverie was broken by a car passing on his right. *This guy must be in a real hurry to pass on the gravel. Why wouldn't he pass on the left? There was no oncoming traffic. Geez, some people just don't know how to drive.* He turned to check out the idiot in the white car flying past. The driver's seat was empty. *Wait a minute! It's me!* The coupe sped downhill, bouncing on the rutted shoulder, passing up the tow truck like it was standing still. He watched her speed toward the curve at the bottom of the hill.

"Oh, shit!" came out almost in a squeak.

He sped forward, realizing all he could do was intercept the coupe by passing it and letting it run into the truck, or pray that she stopped on the next uphill.

The little, white runaway reached the curve where the road disappeared to the right around a clump of trees and kept going straight. John watched her career over the side of the road, disappear momentarily, and then reappear on the flatland below the road leading up to an old cemetery. She rolled across the short field and smacked into a headstone. The car bounced on impact.

John reached the spot where the Ford left the road and hurriedly pulled over onto the opposite shoulder, tires slipping on gravel.

The coupe had found the side entrance of the memorial park, sitting at the bottom of a steep decline where no gate limited access. John scurried out of the truck and slipped down the hill where clumps of frozen snow hugged the tall, brown grass and sparkled in the morning sunlight. The coupe's front bumper bore a modest dent; the headstone had not fared as well. The whitewashed stone tablet tipped sideways, a substantial crack ran halfway through its face, and the earth bulged at the opposite side of the blow.

He glanced up to the road where the tow truck sat, down at the coupe, then back to the road. Getting the Ford up there meant maneuvering the truck down the bank and back up again. The ground was slick with crusted snow. Even on dry earth, it would be risky. He certainly did not want to damage Pop's tow truck. What about entering the cemetery through the main gate? That might work, though it would be tight driving between the headstones.

John ran up to the road and down to the narrow entrance drive, his heart pounding. He might make it home in time after all. A black, cast-iron fence stretched protectively along the memorial park before the road curved and banked, centered at the entrance by a double gate of swirling iron reaching five feet high. John gave the gate a push. It moved only slightly then resisted against the large padlock holding it shut. No getting in this way.

He dropped his head against the cold, metal gate in defeat. He would have to call Pop for help. Plodding toward the truck, he thought about what he would say.

The Olds slid onto the shoulder, and then Pop silently exited. He walked down the hill. No words were exchanged; he had said what he wanted to over the phone. Stealing the tow truck and damaging property? Pop said he should call the police and let them deal with it.

Pop stood silently and surveyed the damage, running his hand over the stone's cracked surface.

Grace Norton
1822–1894
May She Rest in Peace

John stood guiltily aside, waiting for Pop to ream him out again. He saw Pop's shoulders shake and his hand lift to his face. *Oh no, he must be really upset.* John had never seen Pop cry. Did he know this Grace Norton? His shoulders shook harder, and then he could hold back no longer. Pop let loose a belly laugh that doubled him over. Hanging onto the headstone for support, he slid to the ground, tears streamed down his cheeks, and his voice choked with laughter. John watched wide-eyed.

"Fifty-seven years of rest and then, then Powerhouse came along." He lifted himself up and patted the tombstone. "Sorry, old girl."

He dabbed his eyes with his red kerchief, sobered himself, and looked at the coupe and said, "Has this thing got a hand brake?"

John nodded.

"Good. Help me out, here."

The two pushed the coupe slowly backward and away from the stone, then John set the brake. They righted the stone and tamped the dirt back into place. Pop returned to the coupe, lay on the ground, and surveyed the underside. "Here's your problem. The undercarriage is rusted; tow hook broke through the rust." He grunted and righted himself. Reaching into his trousers pocket, Pop pulled out a skeleton key and handed it to John. "Go unlock the gate and I'll bring the truck around."

"How did you get this?" John was incredulous.

"I called a customer who works at the courthouse—got him out of bed. A few phone calls later, and he gets back to me with the address of the township groundskeeper who has a key."

John smiled at his hero, the one who knew how to handle anything. Pop smiled back and gave a playful slap upside John's head.

"Get going. You don't want to upset your mother."

Eight ten. Everyone would be up by now, but there was still the chance he could sneak into the house without being seen. John stood against the house, out of sight, and gradually peered through the white, cotton sheers draping the front window. Good. They were already in the kitchen—behind the swinging doors. The family always ate breakfast at the little dinette in the kitchen. Beneath the doors' opening, he saw Momma's legs travel from the counter to the table. He turned back with a relieved sigh, pressed against the siding, and jumped with a start to see someone staring at him from across the street.

Old man Miller stood peering out his front window at the Powers residence. That old kook. What was he doing up early on a Sunday morning staring out his window at the neighbors? Mr. Miller had some strange psychological problem that rendered him terrified of leaving his property. He lived alone and had his groceries delivered, never walking past the end of his driveway.

John gingerly slid his key in the doorknob and slowly opened the front door enough to squeeze his lank frame inside. Soft voices and the clink of silverware on dishes emanated from the kitchen. He pushed the door silently shut and quietly but quickly ascended the stairs. In his haste, he forgot about the two creaking steps.

"Johnny, is that you?" Momma's voice carried from the kitchen.

"Yeah," John quickly turned to come back down the steps, tousling his hair.

The smell of warm pancakes and maple syrup wafted past as he entered the kitchen, yawned for effect, and plopped at the table.

Susan's large eyes smiled at him over her glass of orange juice.

"Oversleep again, son?" Dad asked. "You know, you have an alarm clock for a reason."

"Sorry, I shut it off and fell back asleep," John lied.

Momma piled several cakes on his plate and handed it across the table. "It's a common teenage problem," she reasoned. "Blanche and Mary at church are always telling me how they can't get their sons out of bed in the morning, and Mary read an article about how teenagers need more sleep for their development."

Dad just shook his head. "Sounds like just plain laziness to me."

"Now, Patrick," Momma cajoled, "leave him alone. Then, shaking her fork at John, she said, "and don't you even think of wearing that to church, young man!"

Johnny smiled and stuffed a forkful of syrup-soaked pancake in his mouth.

Chapter Three

"HEY, POWERHOUSE," POP CALLED from the office doorway, "you got time to do an oil change on Mrs. Saunders's Chevy?" John rolled out from underneath the truck he was greasing and peered through the fogged glass of the wall clock.

"Yeah. Pull it in and I'll get to it in a couple of minutes." Mrs. Saunders would have to be his last customer. It was almost noon and he had both an essay to finish and a geometry test to study for by dinnertime. Then it would be back to the garage to work on the Ford. Typical Saturday stuff: work with Pop in the morning, do homework in the afternoon, eat dinner, then work on his baby until about 11:00. Having a key to the garage gave him the freedom to come and go whenever he could squeeze it in, except on

Sundays of course. It about drove him crazy that Momma wouldn't let him go to the garage on Sundays.

John finished with the truck and walked out to greet his next customer, a requirement for anyone working for Pop's. "How are you today, Mrs. Saunders?"

Mrs. Saunders, all of twenty-two, glowed in a yellow cotton dress that caressed her breasts and flowed softly over her hips to stop just at her shapely calves. Her pale blond hair smoothed perfectly to her shoulders and curved under, shimmering in the late morning sun. She was the loveliest creature John had ever seen in the flesh, and she was standing so close that John caught the scent of her perfume.

"Just fine. And starting right now, you must call me Maggie. Isn't it a beautiful spring afternoon! I brought some cut lilacs for the front counter. They smell heavenly."

John wiped his hands on a clean rag and struggled to keep from looking at the pair of firm lemons in front of him. Her dress was modest, but the fit left little to the imagination. He felt himself harden and was glad for the large coveralls he wore over his street clothes.

"That's great. We could use a woman's touch around here."

"I'll say." She lifted white-gloved fingers to the brim of her hat and, turning her face slightly away, allowed her eyes to run the course of his body. "How old are you?" she asked.

"Seventeen," he lied. It was close enough. Sixteen sounded too young.

"Ah. Well. Hmmm." She chuckled softly. "You could pass for almost twenty. Has anyone ever told you how good looking you are?"

John flushed.

"Not exactly, no."

"She's all set!" Pop called from inside the garage.

"I'm running a bit late today, so I'd better get at it." John felt a strange mix of relief and hesitation to exit the conversation.

"Sure, sweetness. You go right ahead." Her red lips parted in a broad smile.

Pop called from within the garage. "Be sure to pick up your glass before you leave. You get one free with every oil change."

"You mean the Libbey glass that I saw on the counter, the one that says, 'Pop's Garage'? I'll be sure to do that," she called back in a friendly tone.

When Pop was out of earshot, John heard her comment mockingly in a low voice, "That will look lovely with my kitchen décor, I'm sure."

John grinned at her comment as he lay back on the creeper and slid under her light blue Chevy to drain the oil. Usually, customers sat in the waiting area inside the office. Yet from his position under the car, John noticed the pair of slender feet elegantly tipping into bone-white stilettos at the other end of the Chevy. She ignored him when he rolled from underneath the vehicle and stood to replace the oil filter.

Each time John peered around the hood to catch a glimpse, he saw her looking off into the trees beyond or at the diner across the street, shifting her weight to and fro. He slowed his pace. Oil poured like honey into the funnel as his eyes studied how the hem of her dress caught the sunshine and fluttered on the breeze like a yellow swallowtail butterfly. Was it sinful to look at another man's wife in such a way? How could he help it, the way she flaunted herself, the way she came at him? He knew she was pursuing him, and it made his heart pump faster and his mind jumble with the possibility of it. Until he noticed his hands soiled with grease and oil. John imagined his greasy hands grabbing her cotton lemons and dirtying her pale hair and demure face as he pressed his lips hard against hers. The thought brought him back to reality.

A woman like her wouldn't be interested in me, anyway, he thought, returning the oil cap to its place and lowering the hood.

With the clunk of metal to metal, she turned and looked at him, watching as he stripped off the soiled denim coverall and hung it on a peg by the workbench. He caught her eye and stood tall, his white T-shirt glowing from the back of the garage. For a moment the two stared at each other—he blank and expressionless and she taunting with lapis-blue eyes under perfectly shaped brows—until she smiled, tilted her head, and dramatically sauntered toward the office out of sight.

"If you don't mind, Momma, I'd like to walk." Marilyn looked up at her son, now head and shoulders above her, stopping the stream of parishioners descending the steps of The Living Waters Methodist Church.

"Walk! It will take you a good hour to get home from here. Why not ride with us?"

How could he tell her it embarrassed him to ride in Dad's ancient Ford, tagging along like a kid in the backseat?

How could she understand that he was ready to explode from restrained anticipation of the summer ahead?

"Let him go, Marilyn. It's a nice day," Dad cajoled as he took her arm.

"Be home by four. I won't have you missing supper," she insisted.

"Home at four," Susan repeated her mother's words for emphasis and shot a crooked smile at John.

He watched his parents walk toward the parking lot, Susan ambling behind in the jerky gait that made her shoulder-length tresses sway despite being captured with a plastic barrette behind each ear.

Susan adored her brother, bonding to him since she had been a pudgy toddler. When they were younger, Susan would tire easily, getting winded playing hide-and-seek or tag in the yard. So when John's allowance came due and he could afford to splurge on a sundae at Woolworth's, Susan enjoyed the piggyback ride or wagon trip into town. It had made him feel good, promising a treat to his little sister, and her excitement added to his pleasure. Pudgy arms draped around his neck, fingers grabbing at his shirt, suede hush puppies bouncing at his side, Susan laughed and talked the entire four-block walk to Main Street.

"Gidd' up, horsy!" John would rest once or twice on the way. Susan was small for her age so easy to carry. He thrived on her joyfulness and the gawking stares from strangers. They were an extraordinary pair, this tall boy of twelve with a round-faced child on his back. Perhaps people were put off by Susan's huge, green eyes blinking from behind gray, cat-rimmed glasses or her thick slurring speech, symptoms of her Down syndrome.

John liked the fact that Susan was different. He knew why Susan made people stare then look away, ignoring her, pretending not to see. Her flaws were obvious—outward and exposed—a reminder of the inner flaws the perfect work so hard to keep out of sight. The stares and whispers from passersby made him love his little sister even more. To John, she was perfect on the inside. God had decided to make her imperfections transparent; that was enough for her to bear.

Her value had burned into his consciousness when they had almost lost her on a steamy summer afternoon when John was ten years old. Returning home from the baseball diamond, John heard his mother's sob-wracked voice raging at a man and woman hastily descending the porch steps. You'll never take my baby away! Never!"

From inside the house, Susan wailed, huddled in a ball in the corner of the kitchen. Even Johnny's cajoling, promising to give her the leather bag of pretty marbles she loved so much, offering to push her on the swing, would not quiet her.

John heard the story when Dad came home from the steel mill. Susan would not be able to enter kindergarten that fall, as she was considered "uneducable." The school board had recommended Susan be institutionalized in a home for "mongoloids," as she would never be able to function in a public school setting. "Send her away and forget," they had said. "It will be the best thing for her. You can have other children who are normal." Her intelligence and spunk had proven them wrong. Just like the song in church, she was the banner of bright colors waving for all to see.

With several hours of freedom stretching before him, John still found himself walking toward the garage. He would just take a quick look; he couldn't go a day without thinking, planning, visualizing. He walked slowly, coveting the new 1951 models that occasionally passed by, envying the drivers their ownership of such fine machines.

He stopped in Sal's diner for a meatloaf sandwich and a Coke to prolong the afternoon. From his seat in the front booth, he could see Pop's Garage across the street. She was in there, his entry to a life he had dreamed about since Dad had taken him to the first NASCAR strictly stock race at Charlotte Speedway in '49. While other kids collected baseball cards, John followed the NASCAR stats as Red Byron and Lee Petty battled for first place. The '40 Ford made racing tangible, as though it could really happen, tucked away in a womb of possibility. It was unseen from anyone outside, covered in a tarp of secrecy and away from prying eyes.

He bit into his warm sandwich, watching the sun sparkle against the red-lettered sign in front: "Pop's Garage, the best service, the best price." The office sat clean and empty, a line of chrome-framed chairs cushioned with crimson Naugahyde behind the wall-length window. John knew Pop was proud of his business; it was the most important thing in his life. Perhaps the Powers family was more important. No, on further contemplation, John determined what meant the most to Pop, at least right now. It was him, John Powers, his youth, and his gumption to do what Pop had wanted to do over a decade ago.

Things were different then. There was the money, the stigma that racing was full of lawless moonshiners, his age, and the time away from a business he was trying to keep running. Perhaps his customers would stop coming if they knew. Pop had a string of excuses for not doing what he really wanted to. That's all they seemed to John, excuses, and poor ones at that. If a person had a desire so tough it penetrated the shield of daily responsibility, playing like scenes from a movie over and over until his heart pounded just from the thought of it, then he should *make* it happen. To hell with what other people thought. There would be no excuses with him. He would do it for Pop—he would do it for his own sanity.

Bells chimed in welcome as John entered the shop's dark front office and locked the door behind him. Soles squeaking across shining black linoleum, he reached the door to the garage and peeked through the window. There she sat, his 1940 Ford coupe, full of beautiful, hopeful possibility. Restoration took what little savings John had and most of his paycheck, even with Pop getting the most expensive parts at cost and donating his labor. The engine was new: a V8 flathead that he and Pop had lowered from a pulley in the ceiling, straining and finessing until perfectly in place, kissing the trans.

With new headers, carburetor, driveshaft, and exhaust system, she was almost ready for bodywork. Not that she had to look pristine to race. John didn't want to look like a novice on the track; yet showing up with a rust bucket wouldn't be great for his image. She had to be ready to race by July. A nice body was secondary.

John entered the garage and pulled the wrinkled cotton tarp over his project. No sense leaving Pop to cover her before opening in the morning. He liked the secrecy, that no one new, not even his folks.

Anonymity would be short-lived. It was already May; soon he would have to tell them his plans.

Dad's laugh carried on the breeze as John approached the house. Only fifteen minutes late. Momma never had dinner on the table when she said anyhow, always fussing over some last-minute detail. John didn't understand why she fussed so and felt sorry that she did not have a daughter who could share her interest. He knew Momma would have liked a daughter to teach the intricacies of womanhood to, someone who would care about on which side of the plate to put the fork and what color damask napkin would match the pattern in the tablecloth. Susan could help some, but she would never mature to the place of understanding that Momma longed for.

Increasingly unable to adjust to Susan's handicap, Momma seemed wearied by the perpetual child that Susan would always be. How could she not be jealous of her friends with daughters entering young womanhood, learning how to wear makeup and walk in heels, preparing to enter high school? John helped out when he could, but he had lost interest in helping his mother in the kitchen by the age of ten. Momma seemed almost a stranger to him now, practicing the art of small talk when appropriate and asking premeditated questions in an effort to keep tabs on his life. He knew it bothered her that she was losing control, releasing her son to a place she knew little about: manhood. He read it in her down-turned face and sad eyes.

Pop sat on the porch with Dad. He no longer needed an invitation to these Sunday feasts; he had become part of the ritual. In warmer weather, the pair sat outdoors in faded green ladder-back chairs creaking with every move, the husky, sweet scent of tobacco rising from Pop's pipe. When the weather turned cold, they retreated to the parlor and swallowed black coffee from Momma's best china. Even during the week, Pop often stopped by for conversation or to listen to the radio news broadcast or the more subdued *Truth or Consequences* show.

John honored these conversations between Pop and his father and left them alone to revel in the latest story or reminisce about the past. These visits were Dad's only opportunity to converse with another man, other than at church or the mill, neither sufficient to satisfy his need for social interaction. For a few hours during the week, his usual boredom and sullenness were brushed aside. His voice rose with enthusiasm and swelled with laughter as he and Pop remembered earlier times or grew agitated when discussing Truman's doctrine on battling communism. Pop brought out youthfulness in Dad that had slowly drained away from years of repetitive obligation and lack of expression.

The men silenced their laughter and watched John walk up the driveway.

"Where've you been, son?"

"Just around town; took my time."

"Must've taken the scenic route." Dad pointed to his watch. "Your mother's been out here on the porch about five times in the last ten minutes." Pop gave his usual broad smile and the two men chuckled as John opened the screen door, rolling his eyes at them in response.

"Where are your manners?" Dad's words stopped John before entering the house. "Say hello to Ted." John turned to see Mr. Miller, who was parked in his rocker on the porch, solemnly gazing at the little group of men across the street.

"Hey, Mr. Miller," John called as he waved. Mr. Miller stood, responded with a quick nod, and sat back down. Dad commented under this breath.

"One of these days, we'll get him to cross the street. It's a personal goal of mine."

"Hmmm. Good luck," Pop muffled over his pipe.

"Oh, there you are!" Momma stepped from the kitchen, still in her church attire, fingers picking at the knot in her turquoise chiffon apron. "Help me pour the lemonade, John. Dinner's almost on the table."

He did as asked while his mother placed pot roast drenched in au jus, whipped potatoes cradling a pool of melted butter, and salad on the table. John savored the scent of the food. It had only been a few hours since lunch, yet he was starving. He seemed hungry all the time lately. He loved his mother's cooking, particularly her homemade rolls, hot and soft with just a touch of sweetness. They wrapped around his soul like a hot bath on a cold night.

"Tell your father we're ready," she said as she breathed in relief and took her seat. She fell into it, rather, and stared blankly at the table.

John noticed the whiteness of her face and the perspiration barely visible on her skin. She looked tired today. *Perhaps*, John thought, *it's just because she's getting older*. He had just never noticed before. It alarmed him to think that Momma, only forty-three years old, would be aging.

"I heard," Dad said as the two men entered the small bungalow and took their seats.

"Pot roast. My favorite!" Pop exclaimed.

The group took hands as was customary and Dad offered a prayer of thanks for the spring day, for continued work at the foundry, for family and friends ...

"And for the best cooking in Pennsylvania," Pop broke in, lifting his lemonade glass for a toast.

Momma blushed through wisps of hair loosened from her updo. Clinking glassware sounded her applause.

"Amen," she proclaimed as she laughed and proceeded to serve up Susan's plate.

"Amen!" Susan insisted on clicking her glass of lemonade with each member. Every ring of the glass caused a soft, hoarse laugh from Susan that sent chuckles around the table.

"Speaking of things to be thankful for," Pop continued, "how about that Ford John's been working on?"

Silence hushed the group as Pop slowly passed the meat platter, all eyes settled on his questioning face.

"They don't know," John shushed. Clearing his throat, he said, "I haven't told them about that yet."

"Oh. Well," Pop began, "I guess ..."

"What Ford?" Momma asked. "Is this a new customer you're helping out?"

"N-n-not exactly," John stammered. He looked for guidance from Pop, who shifted uncomfortably in his seat then quickly regrouped.

"The kid found this used-up '40 and picked it up for a song," Pop began in a tone of hushed anticipation. "The fool who owned it had seized up the engine. It's got some rust, nothing we can't fix. The first thing we did was drop in a new flathead V-8. We replaced the driveshaft and exhaust last week." His voice strengthened as he continued. "John's done most of the work himself. Paid for it too."

"Why do you need a car, Johnny?" his mother questioned. "School and the garage are close enough. You agreed to start saving your money for college."

I won't be driving it to school."

"She's a racecar," Pop broke in. "We're getting her ready so John can join the local circuit in July. By the time we're done with her, she'll do close to a hundred miles per hour; if the kid can handle her, that is."

"Oh, no, John you're not going to race! It's too dangerous!"

"Now, Marilyn," Pop assured, "do you think I would let your boy do anything dangerous? All he'll be doing is driving around in a circle trying to get to the finish line first. Besides, he's a natural. He knows how to handle a car."

"How do you know if he can handle a car? He's only sixteen."

"We've stopped out to the track a few times with my Olds. When it's empty, that is. He's got good control. Who knows? Maybe he'll make Pittsburgh proud by winning at NASCAR like Dick Linder did three times last year.

"I can't believe you two have been planning this all along and haven't said anything," Momma complained. "What makes you think I'm going to let him race? He's too young."

"*He'sth* too young," Susan repeated while shaking her head.

"He *is* a bit young for it, don't you think?" Dad spoke for the first time.

"Not really. Skill is more important than age. Fireball Roberts is only twenty-one."

"Fireball who?" Momma shrieked.

"No one will ask him about his age. He looks nineteen or better. Besides, I've had him lifting weights since February so he'll have sufficient upper-body strength to handle the car at top speed."

Momma sighed and threw her napkin on the table. "And when are these races to take place?"

"It varies. Weekends usually. Sunday afternoons. They won't interfere with school or work," Pop assured.

"No, only with the Lord's day." Momma angrily pushed her chair back and hurried into the kitchen. Pop rose from his seat.

"I'll go," Dad responded. He quietly pushed through the swinging doors into the kitchen.

"Isth Momma crying?" Susan asked.

"It's okay, Susan." Pop gave her a soft look and rested a large, freckled hand on hers. "Momma will be fine."

"I'm going to *thee.*" Susan pushed herself from the table and traipsed to the kitchen.

"That went well," John said, stabbing his fork into a chunk of pot roast.

"She'll come around. She's just worried about you turning out bad, chasing around with all those old moonshiners." John smiled at the way Pop could make light of the situation. "Just make sure you keep up your studies and stay out of trouble, just likc you always—well, usually—do. You might even make it to Sunday service before the race. Show her how a real man acts. You hear me?"

"Yes, sir."

Momma returned to the dining table. Dad helped her be seated and pushed her chair to the table. John could tell she had been crying, and it made him feel like a heel.

"No sense spoiling a lovely dinner." Her voice was pleasant and light. "We can talk more about this later on."

"Sorry to have upset you, Marilyn," Pop said. "I've been telling John how important it is to keep up his studies and his church attendance, just like he always has. It's a good boy you have here, a fine young man."

"Yes, I know."

"Well. The food is still nice and hot," Pop assured as he accepted the bowl of potatoes from Dad.

John caught a flicker in their eyes, a silent exchange between the two men in the simple gesture of handing off a side dish that made his pulse skip a beat. In that brief instant, their glance spoke of a common thread where no words were allowed, one thought that dared to rise brief and uncontrollable, a silent cry across the table: "We'll be damned if this one will have to forgo his dreams like we did."

Dinner progressed quietly all the way through the lime Jell-O ambrosia, Momma picking at her food. Susan was the first to break the silence.

"May I be 'scused?" she asked.

"Yes, dear," Mom answered. "Put your plate in the sink and go play in your room. I'll be up in a little while to help with your bath."

"How about if you and I go see this monstrosity you've described?" Dad stood and addressed Pop. "John can clean up for his mother tonight."

Pop grunted from the table and stood up. The two men donned sweaters and walked outdoors into the chilly spring evening.

Momma refused to lift her eyes from the table, but she rose gracefully from her chair and began to clear the table. His father's Ford puttered down the driveway and into the distance, leaving John to handle the fallout alone.

"Let me handle this," John said. "You can rest awhile."

"I'm not tired," Momma snapped back. "I'm fine, and I don't need any help."

John lowered his eyes and followed her into the kitchen, a plate in each hand. They reached the sink where Mom had set the empty platter she was carrying, and John could see the angst on her face. He stood waiting for her to step aside so he could set the plates in the sink.

In a rush of emotion, she flung her arms toward him, knocking dirty plates across the room. They rattled and crashed on the floor. "I told you! I don't need your help! Why don't you go with the men and play with your new racing machine." She started to cry, straining with all her might to hold in her pain.

"Momma."

"Never mind." Then, attempting to hide her eyes behind her thin hands, she said, "I'll clean this up."

"No, Momma, let me help." Mother and son kneeled on the floor to gather broken pieces of porcelain and wipe spilled gravy from the gray linoleum. Trying to lighten the mood, John commented softly, "See, you should have used the melamine plates."

"Not for Sunday dinner," she said, her voice terse. "Sunday is special."

She regained composure at the kitchen sink and placed her apron over her dress, quickly tying the bow behind her back. "I just don't understand why you would keep this from your father and me."

"I planned to tell you. It just wasn't the right time."

"Because you knew I wouldn't approve. Not only is it dangerous, it's immoral to race for money—especially on Sunday. You knew how I would feel about this and you went ahead, behind my back." Her words were calculated, steady, fraught with self-control.

She ran the warm water while John carried the remaining dishes from the table. Her tone soothed as her hands fondled and rubbed dishes in the warm, soapy water.

He had to make her understand. "This is something I've wanted to do as long as I can remember. I want it so bad it keeps me awake at night thinking about it."

"You need to be thinking about planning a future, about college and making a good living for your family," she snapped back, "not about racing around with a bunch of hoodlums."

"There's still time for all that. This is what I want to do now! If I'm good enough, I could make a living at it. Johnny Mantz took home over ten thousand dollars last fall with his Plymouth!"

His mother closed her eyes and lifted her palm toward John as if to shove the words back into his throat and away from her tender ears. "If you start with this," she replied, "with shirking the Lord's day and throwing it in His face, the rest of your life will follow suit. Don't you see that?"

John threw the dishtowel on the counter and took his mothers shoulders in his hands, forcing her to look at his face. "Momma, racing is not an evil thing. It is what I want more than anything. If God cares about me at all, don't you think He would want me to do what makes me happy?"

Momma quietly turned her face away and put the last glass on the drying rack. Silence hung thick in the air, making it difficult for John to breathe. The acceptance he hoped to hear did not come. She could not release her grip on conventionality; it emblazoned her heart with knowledge of how things should be done, even if her son's happiness was at stake.

Finally, Momma let her thoughts spill. "You're only sixteen! When you're not at school, you're at the garage working your life away. Why don't you get involved with sports or go to some of the dances like the other kids? Why don't you ever bring any friends to the house? It's not normal."

So that was it. She wanted a more normal son. One who acted like the majority of bubble-headed teenage guys whose chief concerns were their performance on the football field and when they would next get laid.

"That stuff doesn't interest me. None of those jokers know what they want out of life. They're just wasting their time. I know what I want."

He watched the look of displeasure settle on his mother's face, the expression that made his stomach feel sick from trying to choke down guilt. It angered him that she could affect him that way. He would stop it, right now, and never feel it again. "You're just upset because you can't control my life!" he yelled. "I'm not your little boy anymore!"

Momma straightened and looked into her son's eyes. "No, I guess you're not." Her eyes flashed with anger and stared at the resolute and stern face of her son. Momma looked at John's unchanging expression, her eyes gradually softening and becoming weaker, pulling away from his gaze like an animal being preyed upon by something stronger than itself. "I can't explain how I feel. It's almost as if you are going off to a place where I won't see you again." She shook the thought from her head and managed a slight smile, touching John's cheek with a slender hand. "Isn't that ridiculous?"

"Ridiculous," John assured before walking away.

Chapter Four

JOHN WELCOMED THE DREARY June morning, which was hot, muggy, and hampered by a gray drizzle. Business at the garage was nonexistent, and he could stay inside and focus on his work without interruption. School was done for the summer, leaving free time to work on the coupe and to get in practice time at the track. John taped the stencil he had prepared, the number 23 floating in the center of a large circle, to the door of the shiny, white coupe and pried the lid from his can of black paint.

Pop kneeled at the rear fender, diligently adding, "Pop's Garage—Logan 6-2843" in red.

"All she needs is my name over the door," John commented.

"Yep. Going to use your given name or the one I came up with?"

"I dunno. Do you think Powerhouse is too pretentious?"

Pop snorted. "What's this? Did they teach you a new word in English class? *Pretentious*," he mimicked. "You're going out there to clean their clocks, and you're worried about being *pretentious*?"

"Right, Powerhouse it is. Actually, I think I'll put both names on here, John "Powerhouse" Powers. I'll have to make a new stencil—I'm dangerous with a paintbrush."

"There's some packing paper and empty boxes out back. You might find some dry enough to use if you go now."

John rested his brush across the open can of inky black paint and uncurled his long legs to rise from the cool, cement floor.

The back door creaked open into the warm, moist air, and John scanned the boxes and wads of brown paper stacked against the trash bin. Most of it looked pretty wet already, but he thought there might be some dry in the middle of the pile. He slowly pulled away the first box, wobbly from moisture and filled with soiled and empty oilcans, and reached for another that hid behind the first, filled with clumps of dry packing paper. He slid the box out a few inches when the paper jerked and let out a sharp yelp that made John jump back.

When he regained composure, he reached for the papers and pulled the uppermost clump away. Underneath, curled among the paper in a desperate attempt to stay dry, lay a small, black dog. It was no bigger than John's size 10 shoe and black except for russet paws and muzzle and two little, round dots where the eyebrows should be.

"Look at you!" John laughed. The puppy whined and pleaded with shiny, black eyes. "Is it just you or are there more in there?"

John quickly pushed aside the few remaining boxes and paper. There were no others—only this one solitary lost soul, shivering from fear. John stroked the soft, black fur and smiled at the feel of a warm, little body, a heartbeat pulsing against his palm. A rear foot lifted and tried to scratch behind an ear, but the paper was too unstable and the pup rolled in the process.

"Got an itch, girl?" John scratched behind the pup's ear with his long fingers. She stilled and gazed on his face with a look that said, "How did you know?" Immediately, the tail end wagged and a little, pink tongue licked John's hand. He found himself laughing out loud. On an impulse, he lifted the pup to his chest and kissed the top of her head. "Let's get you in where it's dry," he cajoled. Then, remembering that puppies do have leaks, he put her back in the box and lifted it under one arm.

Pop stood next to his work of art, rubbing red paint from the tip of his brush onto a turpentine-soaked rag. "Did you find a good one?"

"I found more than that. Take a look." John lifted the box under Pop's nose and pulled away the loose paper.

"Well, I'll be!" Pop pulled the pup from her hiding place and lifted her up in his large hands—one supporting her chest and the other behind her rump. He turned her from side to side and every way but upside down. "She's a Rottweiler."

"I've never heard of a Rottweiler. How big do they get?"

"Pretty big. Make good guard dogs. Where's your momma, little girl. Huh?"

"So, you're sure it's a girl?"

Pop shot John a smirk and held the pup out for inspection. "Yes, I'm sure. Wanna check?"

"What should we do with her?"

"Keep her. Why not? She can be our watchdog, unless you want to take her home. You found her, after all." Pop held the pup close to his chest with one arm and rubbed her ears.

"No, are you kidding? Momma would never let a dog like that in the house. But why keep her here? You can take her home with you."

Pop shook his head. "She'd be alone too much. I'm here more than I'm home, and so are you. No, we'll set her up with a bed, food, and water, and I'll take her home on Sundays."

"Shouldn't we try to find out who she belongs to?"

"No." Pop was adamant. "Someone who dumps a pup in a trash heap doesn't deserve her. She's ours now."

"What do you want to call her?"

"You come up with something."

John pondered for a bit, and then he noticed the lettering on the side of the box she had chosen for her shelter. "How about Libbey?"

"Hey, Libbey! You hungry?" Pop handed his warm bundle to John. "Here. Get her some water and find her something to eat. I've got a salami sandwich in my box she can share."

John carried Libbey into the front office and set her on the floor. While she investigated her new surroundings and piddled against one of the Naugahyde chairs, John found a clean hubcap for water and pulled a meatloaf sandwich from his lunch bag. He tore half of the sandwich into pieces, placed it on the bag, and set it on the floor next to the counter. Libbey ran toward it with a happy yelp and started gobbling.

"Slow down, girl!"

The welcome bells jangled as a suited man and a young lady entered and approached the counter.

"Can I help you?"

"Yes, I'm here to pick up my Buick. The name's Grant."

"Finished it yesterday, Dr. Grant. Let me pull it around for you."

Good. Libbey was still eating and should be preoccupied long enough for him to pull the car to the front door. He signaled to Pop that a customer was waiting to take care of his bill and lifted the large door to the third service well. The drizzle had stopped and a bit of blue sky struggled to gain control against the clouds.

John turned the key in the Roadmaster and eased it out of the garage and to the front door, leaving the engine running.

He entered the waiting area to find Libbey happily resting in the arms of Dr. Grant's daughter. "She's so precious!" she piped. "What's her name?"

"Libbey."

"Oh, how perfect." The girl looked familiar to John, but he couldn't place where he had seen her. He noticed how her brunette pageboy framed her pale-skinned complexion, her dark-blue eyes, and cherry-red lips. Red, white, and blue: an all-American girl.

She crinkled her nose and rubbed it against the puppy's cheek. John was struck by the lush, dark lashes framing her eyes that smiled with liveliness and made him want to laugh out loud. She exuded happiness and energy. Where *had* he seen her before?

"And what's your name?" John asked.

"Helen. Helen Grant. Nice to meet you." She shifted Libbey to one arm and held out a gloved hand. It rested as gentle as a bird in John's grasp.

"I'm John Powers."

"I know. You were in my chemistry class last year. You sat in the front row so you probably never saw me way in the back."

"No, no. I remember seeing you."

"Time to go, Helen." Dr. Grant had paid his bill.

Helen handed Libbey to John and her father locked eyes with him, lifting his fingers to the brim of his hat in a brief acknowledgment.

"Thanks for your business," John said.

"Thank you. We'll be back."

"Bye, precious." Helen blew a kiss to Libbey and followed her father to the waiting Buick. "Good bye, John. See you in the fall."

He imagined her smiling eyes looking for him among the rows of desks and felt thick, soft warmth expanding in his chest. He watched the midnight-blue Roadmaster turn slowly into traffic and glide down the road until it was out of sight. Helen. He'd have to remember her name so he could say hello the first day back. Perhaps he would keep an eye on her for the senior prom. If nothing else, it would make Momma happy.

"You know her?" Pop questioned.

"No, not really. She's just someone from school."

"Seems like a nice girl. You're mother had a laugh like that."

John spent the next two hours painting the finishing touches on his racer and trying to keep Libbey out of trouble while Pop stepped out for supplies. Finally, Pop returned with dog food, a pair of dishes, a leash, a collar, and a bed large enough for a Great Dane.

"Don't you think this is a bit large?" John sneered as he held up a twelve-inch collar.

"That's for later. She'll grow into it."

"You forgot something," John commented, rummaging through the shopping bag. "She's a baby—she'll need something to chew on."

"Hmmm." Pop disappeared into the front office and returned with a handful of new rags and a plastic promotional truck donated by the local Chevy dealership for display.

"You don't want her chewing on that!" John admonished and grabbed the truck.

"Why not? It's worthless, and it'll give her something to play with until I can bring her a bone."

The '40 Ford was left with drying paint while Pop and John drove the Olds to Mercer Raceway Park, less than an hour's ride north, for a practice run. Mercer was brand new and less crowded than the established Canfield Fairgrounds, about the same distance south, or the popular Heidelberg track at the outskirts of Pittsburgh. Pop had heard about the new track from his Pennzoil dealer who created the Mercer Raceway to give locals the same excitement found at the Canfield and Sharon speedways in nearby Ohio.

The track manager took John's money for a half hour of track time. Mercer was still closed to the public, ideal for learning the nuances of the oval. Approaching the track, John noticed two Fords parked just outside the dirt oval and splattered with dried mud. The drivers stood nearby; a small, twenty-something, dark-skinned fellow in jeans and leather boots handed a wad of crumpled bills to an older man with shortly cropped dirty-blond hair. The older man, probably thirty-six years old, nursed the stub of a cigarette in the corner of his mouth and counted his money.

The younger poked the toe of his boot into the dry, graveled earth and mumbled dejectedly. "I don't understand it. She just didn't' have any get up out there. I beat four of 'em last week clean."

"Well, better luck next time." The older man gave a brief, slanted grin and handed a bill back to the younger. "Maybe you should learn to tighten down those curves. That's your biggest problem—too sloppy at the curves, and almost a half-mile of track. The curves'll come at you fast on a quarter mile." He ground his cigarette butt into the gravel and eyed the approaching Olds.

Pop parked on the track and surrendered the driver's seat to John. He slowly walked to the outside edge of the track and pulled a dulled brass stopwatch from his pocket.

The blond bystander approached and stood at Pop's side. "Nice of you to let the kid borrow your car."

"Thanks. His is still in the shop."

John drove the Olds around the track once and parked at the starting line—kicking the gas. Pop held the stopwatch over his head, thumb in position, and waited.

The Olds roared ahead, dust and gravel kicking up from her wheels, as Pop brought the stopwatch down.

John handled the first turn well, hugging the outside corner and cutting down out of the curve, passing unseen opponents. He gained speed at the far straightaway, a slight downhill to turns three and four. Turn three had been cut in during development to avoid a natural spring, giving the oval a strange D shape.

Pop clicked the stopwatch as the Olds sped past, completing the first lap.

The lone spectator looked over Pop's shoulder. "Just over fifteen seconds. Let's see, that should be about …" He squinted. "Sixty-five miles an hour. Not bad for a kid just out of driver's training." He thrust his hand toward Pop, "Murphy. Frank Murphy."

Pop shook Murphy's hand as the Olds approached the last turn of lap two. "Excuse me, I have to pay attention …"

Murphy grinned and nodded.

Pop continued. "He usually picks up some speed after the first few laps." Pop clicked the stopwatch as the Olds roared past the men for a third time, mere feet away, emitting a deafening growl.

"I'll be damned," Murphy said as he peered at the stopwatch. "You're right."

Pop nodded.

"So, has the kid ever raced, or does he just run time trails?"

"Not yet. I wanted him to get a good handle of the track before …"

"Well, there's a first time for everything!" Murphy was already headed for his Ford.

Before Pop could protest, he revved the engine and pulled the Ford toward the track. John, just past the fourth curve, raced down the straightaway.

A considerate driver would have waited for him to pass then attempted to catch up. Not Murphy. He charged onto the track in front of the Olds. Startled, John swerved toward the inside to avoid hitting the Ford, overbearing slightly on the wheel, barely maintaining control of the Olds on the dirt surface.

Pops shielded his eyes from gravel spit up from the tires.

Murphy gunned it to catch the Olds as it sped by.

"What are you doing?" Pop yelled from the sidelines. Under his breath, he said, "Idiot."

Murphy chased John until he caught him along the far straightaway, both cars side-by-side, the Olds struggling to maintain the lead.

Pops watched as they approached the curve, holding his breath. John slid toward the outside as he had always done. "Slow it down. Slow it down," Pop breathed. This time, there was a tank of a Ford in the way. John took the curve with brakes on, sliding straight toward the outside edge then turning too fast coming out of the turn, skidding out of control—flying dust impeding Pop's view. The Ford swerved as smooth as butter around the rocking Olds, slicing through airborne dirt.

Murphy slowed at the straightaway and pulled off the track. John slowed just enough to regain control and hurriedly pulled off the track behind Murphy. Eyes wild, he jumped from the car before Murphy had even opened his door.

"What the hell were you doing out there?" he hollered. "Trying to run me off the track?"

"Whoa, boy." Murphy exited his car and removed a pack of cigarettes from his rolled shirtsleeve. "I was just trying to teach you how it's done." He tapped a cigarette loose from its box and, perching it between his thin lips, struck a match.

"Great way to go about it! I didn't even see you until you were on top of me."

"That was your first mistake. Do you want to hear about the rest?"

"Not from you. Who do you think you are anyway?"

Murphy extended his hand. "Murphy's the name. Welcome to the world of stock racing, kid."

John crossed his arms over his chest and walked toward Pop, eyeing Murphy as if he were a rabid dog. "Come on, let's get out of here," John huffed. "I've had enough for today."

Pop shot Murphy a warning look and, shaking his head, hopped into the driver's seat.

The pair rode in silence all the way to the Allegheny River bridge before Pop finally spoke up. "He's got a point, you know."

John leaned against the passenger door and rolled his eyes.

"You do need to get some runs in with other drivers on the track before we cut you loose. The track should open to the public by the end of July. You need to be in that first race."

"Great. Who am I going to race against—idiots like Murphy?"

A faint grin eased across Pop's face. "I can come up with a more suitable alternative."

"You know somebody? Who?"

Only silence was the response, silence and a gleam of fantasy and youth that sparked in the older man's eyes.

"You?" John continued. "You mean that you'll do it? That's a great idea!" Then, becoming somber again, he said, "What if I clip your Olds?"

"I own a garage. It's fixable. Besides, you won't clip my Olds because I won't let you. Remember: slow down before the turn, not into it. Tires don't brake and turn at the same time. That will help you through the rough spots."

"I know all that, Pop. It's just hard remembering to do it when you're in a hurry."

Pop chuckled.

"When's the last time you raced?"

Pop frowned and let out a long sigh. "Oh, I don't know. '39, I guess. Long time ago."

"Why did you stop?"

"I've told you before why."

"Tell me again."

"I had been getting a lot of flak from the mill. They didn't think it was a good thing for one of their foremen to spend his free time racing. That was before I quit and opened the shop. There was a lot of bad blood in racing then, hard living and law breaking that didn't suit my style. Some of the guys would get crazy and pull stupid stunts on the track. I put up with it for a while."

"Why didn't you say to hell with everyone else and just do it anyway? You could have kept clean, like Red Byron."

"I saw a man die when he ran head on into a spinout. He couldn't get out of his car fast enough. The flames hit the gas tank, and he was a goner. He was a good man with a young family, just in the wrong place at the wrong time. That did me in. Suppose I was a coward. Perhaps I just didn't want it bad enough. Racing for me was a good time. When it wasn't fun anymore, I got out."

John sat upright now, silently taking in Pop's story.

"Do you think it's wrong … wrong for me to want to race, that is?" John finally asked. "I mean, Momma thinks racing is straight from hell, and from what you've just told me, and what happened today on the track …" His voice trailed off then became stronger. "But I feel like I *need* to do this! I think of racing all the time. I see myself winning. I know I can do this."

"Then you have to do it." Pop was matter-of-fact. "Stock racing is more regulated than it was in my day. NASCAR didn't exist until 1947. You have the ability and enough determination; you'll make it. Show up at the garage after church tomorrow, and you can follow me up to the track. I have faith in you."

Pop removed a large hand from the steering wheel and gave John's shoulder a shake. John felt a knot in his throat. His eyes warmed with moisture.

"Thanks. No one has ever said that to me before." He swallowed hard and blinked back any trace of emotion. Glancing at Pop, watching him ease the Olds off the highway, he felt sad for him. Not pity—he respected Pop too much to ever feel pity. It was pain; it was yearning for a dream that refused to lie down and die but imposed itself onto him with a vengeance.

John wondered if he had picked up the desire to race by osmosis, by the multitude of hours spent working alongside this man. If only Pop had an older, wiser friend when he was young, he would have pursued his dreams despite ridicule and fear.

It was settled then. He would do this no matter who complained, threatened, or cajoled. He would pursue Pop's dream, his own dream, no matter what the cost.

Chapter Five

Saturday evening stretched languid and boring. With no work left on the coupe and the absence of schoolwork, John felt jittery and unfocused. He lazed round the house, his chores done for the weekend, until he couldn't stand it any longer.

"I'm heading out for a while. Think I'll hit the diner for a soda," he called to his parents, the screen door banging behind him.

Thick warm air enveloped John as he walked the paved sidewalk into town, passing sturdy brick homes bordered by mature trees, leaves rustling in the evening breeze. A coral sun hung low, gradually descending into twilight. A cricket chirped from the grass, readying for the evening concert. It felt good to be outside. It felt great to be young with the summer in front of him. This summer was his time to enter the racing circuit, to start doing what he wanted to do for the rest of his life. He was bursting to tell someone, anyone, that he had arrived. Right now, he needed to surround himself with other people.

The diner sparkled in silver and neon as daylight waned. John sequestered himself into a back booth facing the door and watched the action. Most tables were occupied, the nearest by a young family. John smiled at their staring son, all of two years old, as he tipped a glass of root beer toward his face.

"Be careful, watch what you're doing," the little boy's mother protested as she guided his hands to avoid calamity.

A young, pink-uniformed waitress appeared at the table. "What can I get you?"

"I'll have what he's having." John pointed to the toddler. "Only larger and with an order of fries."

At the opposite end of the diner, a couple jitterbugged to a swing tune flowing from the Wurlitzer's lighted bubble glass, the music pulsing behind voices and laughter that rose and fell across the restaurant.

John dabbed his fries in ketchup and eyed a group of chattering girls perched on counter stools like a flock of preening parrots, demurely sipping on Cokes, their polished nails as red as their lips. Teenage girls were an enigma to be studied from a distance and approached with caution. Sure, he would like one, as long as she didn't try to wet-blanket his racing career. It would be nice to have someone to hang out with, a girl who was pretty and smart and would have sex. He wondered if Miss Helen Grant would have sex. She certainly fit the other two criteria.

John washed down his last fry with a swig of sweet root beer, unaware of the blue dress that approached his booth and slid into the opposing seat.

"Hi, sweetness. Did Pop cut you loose for the weekend?" It was Mrs. Saunders—Maggie with the pale-blue Chevy.

"Oh, hello. I don't usually work on Saturday night."

"Well then, where have you been keeping yourself? I've never seen you at the normal weekend haunts."

"Around. I've been busy at the shop fixing up my car." John glanced at Maggie's hands, small and pink, resting on the table. Her nails were perfectly shaped and glossed in pale pink—a paint job any body expert would admire. Where was her wedding ring? It seemed odd, her being out alone on a Saturday evening. "Is your husband here with you?"

"No," Maggie snorted. "Bob's in Chicago at a sales conference. He won't be back until Tuesday. He works in Chicago more than he does here. What's wrong with your car?"

"Nothing. I've been getting ready to … It's a racecar."

"A racecar," Maggie cooed. "How exciting! Where do you race?" She thought and then added, "Aren't you a bit young for racing?"

"Well, I don't really race … yet. I'm planning to join the circuit next month, starting up at Mercer when it opens."

"Mercer." Maggie squinted as if trying to picture where Mercer was.

John noticed her glossy, blonde tresses curling in just at her shoulders and the electric blue of her dress. She smelled good, like the sweet, gentle fragrance of Momma's lily-of-the-valley that crowded around the shade tree in springtime.

"Yes, I know where that is. But isn't there a track right near Pittsburgh?"

"Pop thought I should start at a smaller track for my first official race and …"

"Can I see it? Not the track, the car. I've never been to a race and would love to see a racecar up close."

John stalled and eyed his watch. No one had seen the coupe except Pop and his father. He felt protective of it, like an artist felt about his work before it had been perfected.

"It's not really a racecar like you might think of a racecar," he fumbled. "It's a stock 1940 Ford coupe with a few legal modifications."

"Perfect. Let's go." Maggie clutched her handbag and stood abruptly. "It's just across the street, right?"

"Sure." John threw his money on the table and followed Maggie out the door and into the warm darkness, feeling in his pocket for the key that he always carried with him. He wondered if Pop would mind him bringing a stranger into the shop after hours and decided he would not. Maggie was a customer, after all.

The bells jangled in welcome as he opened the front door.

"I should leave the front light off or we might get a customer," he explained.

He led her through the dark waiting area to the door entering the garage. Once in the garage, he flipped on the light. The only car in the large room, the coupe lit up in all her white glory. His heart pounded a little faster just looking at her, his name stretched over the side window frame and the door emblazoned with a large "23."

"Ohhh," Maggie moaned as she approached the car. She rested her hand on the door latch and peered inside. "It's incredible."

John stood back and grinned like a proud father.

"Powerhouse," Maggie said as she giggled, "is that what they call you? I *love* it!" She circled the coupe, eyeing every detail, until reaching the front. "Why are the headlights covered?"

"To protect them during the race. Otherwise, they would crack from gravel thrown up from the track. It's easier than taking them out and putting them back in after the race."

"Oh. That makes sense."

With a willing audience, John sprang to life, explaining the nuances of a stock car.

"In strictly stock racing, you can't modify the car very much. There are regulations limiting what you can do— nothing, really—to increase speed other than remove extra trim." He crossed the garage to the back wall and lifted a fine mesh screen from the workbench. "Like this. We can put a screen over the front grill to keep dirt from clogging the radiator. It's called a shaker." He modeled how the screen would look on the coupe.

"Did you design this yourself?" Maggie asked. She ran her fingers over the screen material. John noticed how she liked to touch everything. He liked that she had touched the coupe—a blessing bestowed while it was still a virgin.

"Pop helped. He's done a lot to get her ready. A lot."

"Is Pop your father?"

"No, just a family friend."

"Oh, I thought since you call him Pop …"

"Everyone calls him that. I don't even know his real name."

Maggie had moved around to the passenger side and was looking at the tire. "No hubcaps either?"

"Nope, though we are allowed to reinforce that right front tire with an extra piece of metal on the wheel well and special bolts. Otherwise, the pull from the constant turns at high speed can rip the tire right off the car."

"I'm impressed, sweetness. You really know your stuff."

"Yeah," John flushed, "I've wanted to do this for a long time. My goal is to race in the NASCAR grand national circuit."

Maggie smiled and nodded. "I like you, John "Powerhouse" Powers. Most people just talk about what they really want and never do anything about it. Or, worse, they don't even let themselves imagine." She was looking at him, a long, intense look right in his eyes that made him self-conscious.

Suddenly she grabbed his wrist and headed for the shop door. "Come on, I want to show you something!"

"What?" he laughingly protested. "Where are we going?"

"Don't ask questions, little boy," she teased. "Just come with me."

They waited for traffic to pass and crossed the street to the diner's parking lot. "Get in," Maggie instructed as she took the driver's seat of her baby-blue Chevy. John reveled in her energy. She had spunk and confidence that girls his age had not yet matured into.

She sat petite behind the large wheel, silent and determined, heading toward the south shore. John lowered his window and slipped his bare arm down the Chevy's side, letting the warm breeze caress his flesh. They followed winding roads to reach Grandview Avenue, flanked by a half-mile narrow strip of park overlooking the Monongahela River.

Maggie parked and, without a word, exited the car and walked to the overlook. John slowly followed. The quiet river glistened more from the moonlight than the lights of downtown Pittsburgh poking through darkness on the opposite shore not a quarter mile away. Just to the left, the Ohio River forked into the Allegheny on the north and the Monongahela on the south. The split created a triangular peninsula with little at its point, swelling into the hub of business, learning, and culture. Across the river sat the cathedral of learning of University of Pittsburgh, municipal buildings, Pitt Stadium, the commerce of Forbes Street, and historical cemeteries and parks. Farther down the shoreline, narrow smokestacks of the steel industry crowded the sky.

Maggie pointed toward the opposite shore. "That is what I want."

"Pittsburgh?" John asked.

"No, silly. I want to own a boutique downtown, somewhere for all the ladies to come for their finest, most beautiful fashions."

"Oh." John pondered.

"You don't sound very encouraging. I've been saving my money since high school, stashing away allowance and grocery money. I'll need money for rent and to decorate and, of course, for fabric and supplies. Bob doesn't even know I have a savings account."

"Why don't you tell him? He has a good job. Maybe he'd help."

"Are you kidding?" Maggie retorted. "Do you know what he did when I told him my idea of owning a boutique? He laughed! He laughed right in my face and said, 'That's a good one, a fashion boutique in Pittsburgh. Maybe in Chicago or New York you could think like that, but not here.' Every time I bring it up, he tells me to just concern myself with running the house and then changes the subject. How can I run a house that's empty? I'll go crazy if I don't get out! I have to have something of my own."

John raised an eyebrow. He agreed with her husband on one point. Pittsburgh was primarily a middle-class, industrial area. Who would buy such finery here? Yet he knew the feeling of longing for risk, for expression outside predictability. He saw his own youthful desire for adventure and creativity reflected in Maggie's eyes.

Maggie continued. "Is there something wrong with wanting to make Pittsburgh a little more beautiful?"

John smiled. "If anyone can do it, you can."

The intensity left Maggie's face and a soft smile emerged.

They stood side by side, staring toward opportunity. The night had turned chilly and Maggie shivered in her silk dress. She headed toward the car, and then hesitated.

"I don't want to go home yet. I've had such a good time talking to you," she said. "What can we do?" When John didn't respond, she continued. "I know! Let's go see your racetrack."

"Mercer? You don't want to drive all the way up there. It's late and I'm not sure I could find it in the dark."

"Let's go see the track just outside of Pittsburgh. Oh, what's it called? Bob has gone to a few races there with clients."

"Heidelberg Raceway," John answered.

Maggie's eyes widened. "That's it. Heidelberg's not far. Let's go."

John eyed his watch. The diner closed twenty minutes ago. His parents would be looking for him soon.

Maggie noticed his hesitancy. "Oh, come on. It's Saturday night—you don't have anywhere else to be." She opened the clasp on her handbag and demurely pulled out her keys, jangling them in front of John. "I'll even let you drive, since I don't know exactly where Heidelberg Raceway is."

John grabbed the keys and hopped into the Chevy.

Highway 28 was all but deserted as they approached the track. The tires crunched over the gravel road leading to the raceway as Maggie pulled a sweater from the backseat and slipped it over her shoulders.

The track was dark and empty. Full trash bins and the smell of fuel oil and hot rubber lingered as evidence of an earlier race. John had never seen an empty track at night, large and foreboding, silent and tempting. He pulled the Chevy to the track's edge. A fleeting urge to pull onto the track and gun it surged through him. John took a deep breath, and let it pass. It would frighten Maggie. It wasn't his car.

Instead, he turned off the ignition and stepped onto the track, rays from the Chevy's headlights streaming before him. Eyes closed, head tilted back, he inhaled the air like a wild beast catching the scent of prey. Standing on the same earth where engines had roared over just a few hours earlier, John felt powerful, even almighty. He would be there soon, contesting with men for the prize of speed, of endurance. He glanced down the darkened raceway, taking it all in, imagining his first race. He saw the spectators lining the track and filling the grandstand, felt the coupe's wheel in his grip, felt her engine rumble through his body, waiting for the green flag, and then the release of ultimate intensity as man and machine became one. The engines growled in his head when a faint female voice broke through.

"John, sweetness, can we go now?" He had completely forgotten about Maggie, who was standing next to the Chevy in her blue dress and high heels. Good Lord, it had been hours since they left the diner.

"Sorry, I was just daydreaming."

"Nothing wrong with that," Maggie said, "as long as you replace those dreams with reality some day."

"Someday is now."

John drove in silence toward home, lost in thought, his soul still lingering over acres of open field surrounding a halo of dirt. Small talk was pointless now. In one evening, John and Maggie had penetrated the first few layers of social strata. They were two strangers intimately connected by an unseen thread of yearning, by a will to create their own future rather than simply allowing it to evolve.

John glanced at Maggie, dozing against the passenger door, her dove-pink skin radiant in the soft dashboard light. He felt protective toward her. What would her husband think if he knew his young wife was out riding around Pittsburgh in the wee hours with another man? When John married, he wouldn't leave town constantly so that his wife had to take the car for oil changes and take herself out alone on Saturday nights.

John smirked. Bob knew Maggie physically, but he was one up on Bob. He knew her dreams, knew she had willingly shared them without fear of rejection. That was the part of Maggie he could claim, could share in as they each entered into a separate future, separate yet now connected. The telling of it was important; lifting what was buried in the mind from obscurity to tangibility. Someone else knew and understood. They would help each other by the knowing. When he thought of Maggie, he would envision her running her own successful boutique, selling evening dresses and shoes to the wives of professors, doctors, and steel magnates.

Pulling into the driveway, John squeezed Maggie's shoulder to waken her. The porch light did its part by glaring into the darkness.

"Are you okay to drive home? I could take you home and walk back."

"Oh, yes," Maggie groaned, "I'm fine. It's a few miles away, too far to walk this late. See, I'm awake now." A soft smile emerged.

John wanted to see Maggie again—he liked her and wanted to maintain their friendship. He couldn't ask for her number, or arrange another meeting, without violating the mores of respectability.

"Thanks for coming to sit with me at the diner. It made my evening a lot more enjoyable." John extended his hand.

Maggie grasped it between her small hands and gave a tight squeeze. "Why thank you, sweetness. I had more fun tonight than I can remember. Will I see you around?"

"Yes. I'll look for you around town."

Maggie, still holding John's hand, leaned over and gave him a quick kiss on the cheek. "You're precious," she said.

John exited the Chevy so Maggie could slide across the seat. He watched her back down the driveway and wave good-bye. Red taillights diminished into two tiny dots in the distance. This mythical creature, this guardian angel who dropped into his booth many hours ago, slowly disappeared into the darkness.

John quietly turned the key in the lock and hushed the creaking front door. The house sat dark and silent. He stood at the base of the stairs, giving his eyes a moment to adjust to the pitch darkness.

His father's voice startled him. "Where have you been?" his voice whispered in restrained anger.

John focused on a shadow of his father's figure rising from his favorite armchair. "Well, I went to the diner and …"

"The diner closed hours ago." Dad was in his son's face now. "It's after 1:00 in the morning."

"That's what I'm trying to tell you. I ran into a friend at the diner and we went to look at the coupe, then …"

"I saw who you were with." His father grabbed John's shirt and clenched it in his fist. "Don't tell me you spent four hours at the garage talking shop."

"No, it's not like that," John protested. "She's married, we were just …"

Dad released his grasp on John's shirt. "So you spent the evening with a married woman," his voice was low and deliberate. "Do you know how worried your mother has been all evening? She's had Pop driving all over town looking for you. Do you have any idea of the lack of respect and consideration you have shown her? Shown all of us?"

"Well, I …"

Smack!

The blow to the side of John's face was forceful enough to send him reeling, his head hitting the front door. He slid to the floor, stunned, his hand covering his burning face.

Dad leaned over his son, physically his equal, and hissed in his ear. "Don't do it again." Then he quietly climbed the stairs to bed.

John lifted himself from the floor, his eyes stinging with tears. Dad had never hit him before, never. His head throbbed from bouncing off the door. John stumbled to the kitchen, filled an ice bag, and slumped at the table. He fell asleep there, forearm for a pillow, ice bag pressed against the goose egg growing above his right temple.

"How was church this morning?" Pop hollered from the garage upon hearing the entrance bells jangle. John hustled through the service door.

"We didn't go. Susan's come down with a bad cold and Momma let me sleep in."

"Late night?" Pop was playing stupid, trying to tease information out of John.

"Yeah, a little." Pop lifted an eyebrow and dropped the subject. Libbey dozed on a large pillow tucked into her own corner of the garage. John reached down to stroke her soft head. She roused and licked his hand.

"You up for this today?"

"Are you kidding?" John retorted. "I've been waiting for this since we first hauled that sorry coupe in here." Pop opened the bay door—his Olds sat outside waiting for its challenger to come out and play.

"I gassed her up this morning. The tools and your helmet are in the Olds—no sense transferring them later."

John started the coupe and eased out of the bay. The new engine rumbled low and steady beneath the glistening, snow-white hood.

Pop shut the bay door after shouting out to Libbey, "See you in a few hours, girl." He hopped into his own car, leading the way to Mercer for a practice race.

John was almost giddy with anticipation, his hands shaking on the wheel from restrained adrenaline. Bright sun gleamed off the coupe and warmed the interior, reminding John to remove the sunglasses tucked in his shirt pocket. Stares, smiles, and an occasional pointed finger accompanied the pair as they rode through town. John felt as if he were a one-man parade and smiled in response.

Once over the bridge and onto the highway toward Mercer, he settled into concentrated thought. *Slow down into the curves. Mash the accelerator on the straightaway.* It seemed to take forever to reach the track; Pop would not exceed the speed limit.

He noticed a new sign posted at the gate: "Mercer Grand Opening: Thursday, July 26—Don't Miss the First Race!" He didn't plan on missing it. July 26 would be his debut, though it was odd to hold races on Thursdays. Perhaps they didn't want to compete against the already established tracks for the weekend crowd. John gave the last of his cash to the clerk, a full hour's worth of track time reserved by Pop the day before, and registered on the spot for a qualification time trial scheduled for the day prior to the race.

"Is there a purse for the top winners?" John asked.

"For the first three to finish, but we don't know how much it will be until race day. Tell your friends. The more admissions we sell, the bigger the purse."

The track was bone dry and empty on this Sunday afternoon. There was no one to wave the flags for this impromptu race. Pop's Olds idled at the pole position while Pop waited for John to settle in, shouting through the opened windows, "When I wave, that's the green flag. Just keep going until I've pulled off the track."

John nodded his agreement and watched from the corner of his eye for Pop's wave. There is was, and both cars roared into motion. John floored the pedal and found his back tires losing traction, spitting up dust, the coupe's rear shimmying sideways. The Olds tore ahead as John grappled with the steering wheel to keep the coupe straight.

"Come on, baby!" He eased on the gas pedal just enough for the tires to grab and pressed again. This time, the tires bit dirt and the coupe lunged forward. John reached the first turn as Pops rounded the second. The urge to catch the car in front of him took over and became John's sole focus. He raced through the second turn faster than he ever had before, barely avoiding a spinout, and came quick on the Olds' tail at the inside base of the curve. John swerved right to avoid tapping the Olds and mashed the accelerator to the floor, watching his opponent disappear from his peripheral vision.

A smile crept over his face. The warm rush of satisfaction that flooded through him at taking first was unmistakable.

Still, he could not back off and risk the Olds regaining its position. He roared up to the third turn, approaching the curve straight on to reach the outside edge from where he would cut down into the curve. This time, the curve came on him too fast; the track's outer edge loomed in front of him as the Ford raced up the bank. He backed off the gas and turned sharp to the right. The coupe couldn't respond to his command, rear tires skidding left until the coupe had spun around and faced the opposite direction, heading down toward the center of the track and the oncoming Olds. A blur of dark blue whizzed past John's window, mere inches away. Finding his bearings, he slammed the gearshift into reverse and backed straight across the track to the outside, turning the coupe back into racing position.

Coming down to the inside, cutting through his own dust, he approached curve four more cautiously and gunned it at the straightaway. Where was Pop? It wasn't until he had rounded the first curve that he realized Pop had pulled off the track. John finished lap two and pulled off as well.

Pop walked up to John's window and leaned against the doorframe to peer inside. "Let's get one thing straight." Pop's face was reddened and intense. "You've got a lot of laps to get to first place. Don't throw out all your horses in the first lap. Drive smart. You were pretty stupid out there."

John nodded in agreement.

"I'm just one car. What would you have done if there were forty others coming at you while you were trying to get your ass turned around?"

"You're right," John answered. "I just got carried away. I know what do to now."

"Good. Shall we try this again?" Pops walked slowly to his Olds, shaking his head.

John surmised what he must be thinking. What had he gotten himself into with this kid who could barely handle the car in the first lap? John couldn't let him down; he had to show Pop that he could do this. Focus. Let the speed come, but focus on the track. Drive like you're the only car out there, and just slip past the others like they are a Burma Shave sign by the side of the road.

John eased back on the track and waited for Pop's nod. He cradled the pedal to full speed and felt the coupe instantly take charge of the track. Focus.

The first curve washed past like a wave, then the second. Pop kept to the middle and inside track. Just as powerful but a heavier car, it was a good contest for a newbie in a Ford coupe. Focus.

The Olds held the lead until the fourth lap. John eased up to Pop's bumper, riding close, waiting to mash the accelerator until within inches of his left tail light, slipping past slowly, slowly. John turned to smile at his opponent, who glanced sideways.

"Don't look at me!" Pop screamed. "Watch the track!"

But John saw the smirk that emerged on Pop's face as the coupe passed and cut in front, forcing the Olds to back off the accelerator. John eyed his mirror, swerving slightly up, then down the bank to keep Pop from passing. He kept the lead for the next five laps by a close margin.

By the tenth lap, track, coupe, and driver melded. John slipped into a place where reminding himself to focus was obsolete. The track became a ribbon that his very breath sailed along, rhythmic and smooth, part of his body, the engine his heartbeat. The straightaways were more forgiving to the Olds, allowing the senior driver to creep ahead in the twelfth lap, inching past the coupe's nose, but not for long. John learned to see the Olds without breaking his stride, saving the top of his speed for when it was most needed.

At thirty-eight rounds, John had lapped the Olds. After forty laps, Pop pulled off the track and John followed. Engines now quiet, the roar still buzzed in their ears, both drivers oblivious to the cluster of onlookers clapping and cheering, happy to have found some free entertainment on a sunny afternoon.

All smiles, the two shook hands and slapped backs. John couldn't remember Pop with so much energy—he was even breathing harder than normal.

"I need to save some rubber for the ride home!" Pop exclaimed as he examined his tires.

"That was pretty good, huh?"

"Pretty good," Pop confirmed, wiping track dust and sweat from his face with a white kerchief.

John smiled with exuberance. This was, by far, the best day of his life. Pop's face said that it might have been up there on his list also. His expression was charged with emotion; controlled elation muddled with the urge to sob. John knew it was because of him. He had given Pop a reason to race again, a reason to care. He wanted nothing more than to fill Pop's life with motivation, to fill him with pride.

"Momma! Don't feel good!" Susan's crying from her upstairs bedroom greeted John home. Mom, frazzled from lack of sleep, stood at the kitchen counter pouring ginger ale into a glass of ice.

"Oh, you're home," she glanced at John. "Take this upstairs to your sister. She's been asking for you all day. Don't let her kiss you; she's got influenza."

John took the tray bearing soda crackers and the glass of pop, started to share his success with Pop on the track, and then stopped. He knew Momma didn't care about that. He didn't want to be harangued and have her spoil his day.

"What?" Her plaid dress was crisp and freshly pressed and her weary eyes were large and deep, yearning for normalcy, for peace. She had missed church, but still she dressed for it.

"Nothing," John answered as he ascended the steps two at a time to Susan's room.

"Johnyyy!" emanated from a mound of covers. Susan's room was minimalist for a young girl with its stark white walls and eyelet lace curtains. A lavender bedspread, a strand of purple beads—the plastic carnival sort—strung over her mirror. Her barrette collection sat on the dresser in ordered rows, each pair organized by color and design: the plastic pink bows lay next to the red flowers followed by little, black Scotties.

John rested the tray on Susan's nightstand, pushing her glasses and several copies of *Highlights for Children* out of the way, and sat on the edge of her bed. Instantly a hot, moist Susan curled on his lap. John pulled the blankets around them to quiet her shivering.

"What happened to you?" John asked.

"Got the flu," Susan whined. "Been throwing up."

"Here, sip on some of this." John handed her the cold glass of ginger ale.

"Where did you go?" Her almond eyes peered into his face.

"Well, remember the racecar I told you about? Today I raced with Pops."

"Did you win?"

"Yep." John squeezed his arms tightly around the blankets encasing Susan's ten-year-old frame.

"Yeah! Johnny won!" She nibbled at a cracker. "Can I see you race?"

"You bet. Save July 26 for me—it'll be our date."

Susan giggled and pressed her round face into John's chest.

Chapter Six

THE ROAD AHEAD GLISTENED under a mirage, ever lifting and moving farther past, as John drove the coupe toward Mercer Raceway. Hot, sticky July air cruised through the open windows and tousled his hair. A smile curved his lips. His first race lay in front of him, now spaced by only a few hours. He had qualified in the time trail as number eight out of twenty-nine and was feeling pretty smug about it. Not a bad place for a first race; he could more quickly advance from eighth to the pole position than the drivers who placed in double digits.

Too bad Pop couldn't be there to see him race. While Pop had hired another mechanic to help with the growing number of clients, all of the bays were full this week and he couldn't get away. Yet a sick feeling swelled in John's gut when he thought about Susan missing the race after he promised it to her. Momma refused to come or to allow Susan to see the race.

"What if you get hurt and Susan see's that?" his mother had said. Why would he get hurt? He knew what he was doing. Besides, Momma was too protective of Susan because of her condition. So what if people stared and whispered? Susan was used to it and didn't care. Momma shouldn't care either.

"You just don't want to take her in public because she embarrasses you," John had accused that morning when told he would be going to the race alone. He immediately felt it wasn't true and wished he hadn't said it. It made his mother sad, and he apologized before leaving the house. He felt relief when he realized the sick feeling of guilt didn't rise up at her tears. He was becoming more of a man now; men couldn't let things like that get to them.

Mercer was a flourish of color and motion. The spectator count was more than he expected on a Thursday afternoon. Every make of car imaginable rolled onto the dirt track and took its place: Ford, Olds, Chevy, Hudson, and Buick. John was amazed that so many men shared his ambition. Walking along the track, gulping Coke from a chilled bottle, he studied the arriving cars and noticed who placed at the pole position. Murphy, the guy who almost ran him off the track, sat in his black Ford while smoking a cigarette and staring at the track, unraveled by the commotion around him. Taking the lead from Murphy would be an incredible feat; a high bar goal for John to strive for.

Good. It gave him a point of focus.

Drivers began to position their cars and Johnny did the same. He watched with interest as the driver in front of him fastened a leather strap, belt-like, around the metal doorframe where it met the post. That would certainly keep the door secure in a crash or rollover. He made a mental note to pick up a few leather straps. Now it was time to focus, to concentrate on one goal: winning. He slipped on his helmet, a rounded hard hat with cloth sections dropping at each side to cover his ears, and strapped it under his chin. Next, the goggles were positioned. A one-hundred-lap race on a dry day would kick up a lot of dust. John felt his heart pounding and his breath grow shallow. *Take deep breaths. Hold it together. Focus.* John turned the key to unlock the ignition and flipped on the ignition switch.

The loudspeaker crackled and whistled before a voice broke through. "Gentlemen, start your engines."

John pulled out the choke and pressed the starter button. A growl rose over the field. He adjusted the choke and gripped the wheel, twisting his hands around it, staring intently through the windshield at the tail end of a black Buick with a large white "8" painted on the trunk. He flashed back to an earlier race on a hot August day in Ohio, the nose of his derby racer resting against the stopper.

"Okay, eight ball," he said, "get ready to roll into the pocket. The cue ball is coming through."

His eyes lifted to the stand and watched for the flagman. What were they waiting for? A flash of green cloth and the huddle of steel lurched forward, following the pace car for one lap as the mass of cars gained speed then let loose.

Come on, eight ball, move your tail! The coupe ran as smooth as butter. There, an opening. John sailed around the

Buick and stayed high into the first turn, dipping down and coming out of the curve to position behind a Pontiac. He gunned the engine, slipping ahead of the Pontiac and cut in front to keep it from regaining a lead with mere inches to spare.

Five laps later, running the inside track, a Plymouth came up on his right, inching toward the lead. John saw it in his peripheral vision, heard the engine gaining. Just enough room between the Plymouth and the car ahead to squeeze through, up, up. He forced the Plymouth back and claimed the high ground just before the curve forced him to back off the gas. The coupe shimmied out of the curve and John fought to retain control and floor it again on the straightaway. He came within a breath's distance of the car that would be his next target, shimming up and down the track until the lead driver was distracted enough from watching his rear to leave the scant possibility of an opening for John to pierce through. *God, this is intense.*

His hands had melded with the wheel, fingers gripping like a steel vise. What position was he? He didn't know. *Just beat Murphy. Get in front of that black Ford.*

The noise was deafening, even with the leather helmet straps over his ears, yet each time John sped past the pole he heard the announcer yelling excitedly into the microphone. Only a few words could be understood.

Within fifteen laps, he entered the zone; man and machine became one. The coupe was the body, John was the brain. Nothing could penetrate the energy, the concentration, which overtook this being. *Win.* Thought and reason moved to a centered place. *Perform.* The white coupe number 23 soared over the track, fighting each car it approached to steal its place, swapping position only twice. When John Powers took the lead over another driver, he usually kept it.

Just when it felt effortless, a spinout ahead sent cars swerving to avoid collision. A red Ford didn't swerve in time and plowed into the disabled car's back fender. John's breath stopped in his chest until he passed the dust and dead steel sitting on the track. *Phew.* He could exhale now. A yellow flag waved over the track and everyone slowed in position until a tow truck cleared the wreck from the track, poor suckers.

Two cars were out of the race and a third was pretty banged up but insisted on limping through. John saw Murphy's Ford several cars ahead, close enough to see his '02 clearly and read "Amoco Gas" on his rear fender when rounding the curve. Three cars to beat to get to Murphy, just three. He could do that.

The coupe slid up alongside the first of three on the inside track, a Hudson, gaining precious inches in the process. The driver spotted the white nemesis and sped just a bit faster. John struggled to keep astride and slowly, gradually, moved the wheel toward the target, forcing the driver to move to the outside track. He stayed at the door, forcing, forcing, until the coupe had willed the car to move out of the way enough to scoot past. John zigged and zagged along the straightaway to keep the Hudson from passing. Realizing the "force up and over" strategy worked, John tried it again on the next victim, a late model Ford. As John approached from the inside, the Ford gave him a battle, cutting down and back up to keep John in his place. At the first curve, John cut it tight and stayed under the Ford, ending up astride as the second curve approached. He stayed close, pushing the Ford toward the outside of the track.

The opposing Ford had two choices: back off the gas and slip behind Powerhouse or stay at pace and move up the track. John glanced aside and saw the driver shouting expletives and struggling to cut back down and in front of the white coupe. John rode astride his front bumper, not letting his opponent move down. Curve number two approached. John stayed tight with the Ford, riding it up the track. Just at the curve's crest, he came down and sped into the straightaway. The other driver was not as skillful coming out of the forced curve and ran off the track, slipping over the side and out of view. John caught sight of the Ford sliding off the track in a puff of dust in his rearview mirror.

"Oops. Didn't mean for that to happen."

He regrouped quickly. Now it was three. All that existed between him and Murphy was a burgundy Mercury, but what a Mercury it was: fast, powerful, countering John's every move with speed and precision. He strained with all his might to get into a parallel position with the Merc, only to ride its bumper up and down the track. Just when he thought he would kiss the Merc's bumper, a rush of power erupted and it moved ahead. John floored the pedal on the straightaways, doing all he could to maintain control at top speed, slowing to handle each curve. The Merc's driver was more skilled. He blocked John's maneuvers and took the curves with more speed and agility. By now, the three lead cars had lapped several others; the stragglers were an annoyance for John as he focused on chasing the Mercury.

Approaching the start/finish line, John heard the announcer's voice rise over the engines. "Powerhouse at third …" Hearing his name gave him a shot of adrenaline. He chased the pair around and around, the Merc swapping the lead with Murphy twice in the process only to slip back. What lap was it? *Don't worry; just keep on.* It seemed forever for John to make it astride the Mercury, riding door to door. Straining, pushing. There! The coupe gained a foot on the Merc's nose.

Murphy's 02 Ford rode just feet in front; John was sandwiched between the Mercury and the bottom of the track. If he could just gain more lead on the Mercury, he could break free.

The racers approached the start/finish line again and John saw the flagman leaning over the railing and waving a pointed finger in the air. One lap to go! His jaw clenched tight, eyes piercing ahead. This was it; he had to stay aggressive.

Inside on the first curve, he had to ease off his speed to avoid colliding with the Mercury, still hovering on his shoulder like a bad dream. Out of the turn, he increased quickly to maximum speed before heading into curve two. The coupe rushed ahead, gaining precious feet on the Mercury whose nose was almost behind John's passenger door. An inch. Another. There! John cut off the Mercury and lifted up to the outside track into the second curve, watching his tail and slowing to avoid tapping the '02 Ford squarely in front of the coupe's bumper. He managed to hold the high ground around the curve and raced along the Ford's flank on the back straight, the Mercury now in his former position.

Too intent to breathe, his hands molded to the steering wheel, the little coupe's engine roared at her top capacity approaching the third turn. The three cars hugged each other around the curve, John intent to keep the Mercury in its place. First place was still within reach—the finish lay ahead. His body and mind strained with everything they had, pushing the coupe along the final straightaway toward the checkered flag wildly flapping at trackside. The Ford pushed harder, a black shadow running along John's side that he couldn't shake. He could have reached out the open window and smacked the '02 painted on Murphy's car.

In an instant, the air exploded with cheering, and it was over. They had passed the finish line. Second! He had finished second in his first run, and the thought made him giddy with pleasure.

Now what? He rode around the track one final lap and pulled off before reaching Frank Murphy's dust, kicked up from the donuts he was cutting in the track. Show off. John was unsure what to do so he turned off the engine and hopped out of the coupe. A swell of cheers and whistles greeted him and caused a choking mix between a cry and laughter to escape from his throat. He removed his goggles and helmet and wiped the sweat from his eyes. His face, even his teeth, felt gritty from the track dust he inadvertently ate.

Frank Murphy had stopped his antics and was talking into a microphone held by the announcer. He heard the voices, yet his mind was too jumbled to make out the words. He saw the announcer hand Frank an envelope and shake hands. A beautiful girl stood with them and kissed Murphy on the cheek. Beyond the starting line, the remaining cars were pulling off the track. He should pull off too. Perhaps he was making a fool of himself staying on the track. After all, he didn't win. Grabbing the door handle, he was stopped by someone calling his name.

"Mr. Powers! John Powers, wait." The announcer and his lovely accomplice were walking toward the coupe, waving John out from behind the car. He did as beckoned. The announcer stood next to the "23" encircled on the passenger door and grabbed John's hand as he approached, pumping his arm with all his might.

"Congratulations! Boy, you're shaking like a leaf! I understand this is your first race. Nicely run; how does it feel?"

John stared back at the stranger dressed in tweed blazer and tie. He wasn't prepared for this. "Good. It feels good."

"I'm sure it does. You gave us a great show out there. For your trouble, you've won twenty-five dollars and a new set of tires, and by the way you raced today, you're going to need them."

John accepted the envelope and a peck on the cheek from the pretty girl with the banner reading "Miss Pittsburgh" draped across her front. He looked into the applauding crowd and felt an overwhelming well of gratitude. These people paid money to see him race—were giving him a new set of tires. So many smiling faces. It felt like waves of affection rolling over him. A camera clicked somewhere. The announcer and Miss Pittsburgh moved off to congratulate the Mercury for winning third place.

John slipped the envelope in his shirt pocket and looked again at the crowd filling the bleachers and standing in clusters trackside. He didn't want to leave this place, not yet. John felt the best he had ever felt in his life. Then he saw what made him feel even better, what made his heart flip and a lump swell in his throat. Standing there on the bleachers was Momma in her Sunday hat and white gloves, and she was surrounded by Dad, Susan, and Pop.

For a moment, the little group and the racecar driver locked their gazes and connected across the multitude of people, Momma waving and Susan jumping up and down. John smiled and waved back.

A photographer approached while lugging a pack full of equipment and a steno pad and pencil. "I'm from the *Pittsburgh Post-Gazette.* Do you mind if I take your picture?"

"No, go ahead!" John stood proud and erect, his hand resting on the coupe's hood, positioning himself so the camera could capture the John "Powerhouse" Powers painted along the crest and the "23" on the side. He squinted in the bright afternoon sun and flashed his best toothy smile for the cameraman.

"Do you have any family here, anyone you would like your photo taken with by the car?"

"Yes, yes I do," John answered. He waved for his parents, Susan, and Pop to come join him.

The group scooted past onlookers to join their hero of the hour for a photo on victory lane. They huddled around John: Pop on one side with his arm draped around the younger man's shoulders, his parents close on the other side, and Susan staring up at her brother as though he had just slain a dragon.

"Susan, dear, turn around and face the camera," Momma said.

Johnny took Susan's chubby hand in his and she strained on tiptoes to reach his ear. He bent down as she quietly spoke for him alone.

"I'm thso proud of my Johnny. *Thso* proud."

Chapter Seven

THE HUNDRED-LAPPER CHEWED SUBSTANTIAL tread from the coupe's tires, but there was enough rubber left on his Firestones to get through another race before cashing in his award. Resting in the shop after her win, the coupe was treated to a wash and oil change, John arriving early Saturday before the customers began to clamor for attention. Racing was going to be expensive. He had already spent the twenty-five dollars for oil, gas, spark plugs, a few leather straps to tie the doors shut, and more practice time at the track. The engine and tires had to be kept in top shape to win, and that took money and time. A set of good tires would easily suck almost two weeks' pay out of his wallet.

His father had been excited after the second-place win at Mercer, treating everyone to dinner after the race, but made it clear that he would not be financing John's new hobby. The word *hobby* was offensive to John, as if his racing were a small-time side stunt for kicks. No one understood how important this was, except for perhaps Pop. Actually, he almost felt as if others were humoring him, going along with his latest whim until it burned out. John didn't mind. He expected nothing less and nothing more. His earnings from the garage and winnings would pay for the Ford's upkeep. He just needed to keep winning, especially since he had shown his stuff at the first Mercer race by taking second his first time out. The spectators would expect to see him back often.

Libbey whined for attention and nuzzled John's hand. In the past six weeks, she had more than doubled her size and become lanky. John stroked her short, black coat and was serving up her breakfast when Pop arrived for the day's work, half an hour before opening to the public. John knew Pop's routine so well he could reenact it in his sleep: maul Libbey for five minutes; step into clean, navy-blue work overalls; tuck a fresh handkerchief in the front pocket; don his dusty and worn conductors cap; fill the percolator with water and enough coffee grounds to brew tar and put it on the hot plate; flip on the front lights; and lift two of the bay doors. Only when these steps were done would Pop acknowledge John and resume the day's work. The other mechanic Pop had hired that summer, Smitty, often showed up about two minutes before opening, gave a quick hello, and poured some thick coffee in his own mug.

This particular Saturday, Pop strayed from his routine. After rubbing down an exuberant Libbey, he walked straight over to John and set the weekend *Gazette* on the coupe's hood.

"Front page of the sports section." Pop pointed to the article. A dark-haired, handsome, young man smiled back at them, leaning against his white coupe. The photo covered half the page. Above the photo, it read, "Local Boy Shows Spunk at First Race."

John snatched the paper and began reading.

"But I came in second," he laughed. "What about Murphy?"

"Oh, he's in there too, see?" Pop flipped the page and pointed to a smaller photo of Murphy with Miss Pittsburgh. "You must be better looking."

Both men laughed at John's instant local fame, at the fact that he had won his first race, albeit in second place, with panache.

Suddenly Pop silenced himself. "Listen, before Smitty shows up, I've been thinking." Pop took the paper from John's hand to regain his attention. Despite their being alone in the garage, Pop spoke in a hushed voice. "You've worked here a long time, always show up on time, and do a good job, and the customers like you too …"

What is he getting at?

"Well, business has been picking up and, frankly you're free advertisement with our name and phone number all over that racecar. They even mention Pop's Garage in the paper. See, right here …"

"What?" John prodded.

"I'm promoting you to manager and giving you a raise. I'm thinking another 50 percent. Now I know it's a lot more all at once, but you've never had one in the several years you've been here and, well, you're approaching adulthood and will have more expenses coming. So I thought now was a good time."

John gleamed at his friend and grabbed his large hand, pumping it with everything he had. "Thanks! You don't know how much … Thank you," he sputtered.

Pop grabbed John's arm with his free hand and gave a hearty squeeze. "You deserve it."

Just then Smitty walked by with his steaming cup of strong coffee, staring at the two in confusion.

"Mornin,'" he said as he nodded.

"Good morning, indeed." Pop boomed, "Look at this! Our friend here has made front-page news." He shoved the paper in Smitty's hand.

"Well, I'll be," Smitty declared. "Look at that. Congratulations, Mr. Powers."

John smiled sheepishly and nodded at the older black man's acknowledgment. He felt suddenly small, being called Mr. Powers by a married man with two kids. Then again, it did have a nice ring to it.

John tapped his pencil on the counter and pondered the statement printed on the Heidelberg Raceway entry form: "Must have a pit crew." He knew Heidelberg was a more formal track than Mercer, sanctioned by NASCAR the year prior. He had to run Heidelberg if he was to achieve the skill and recognition to make his dream of qualifying for the NASCAR circuit a reality. This race was two hundred laps around the half-mile track. He may need to pit for gas during the race or need fresh tires. He had never raced one hundred miles and had not given much thought to backup. Pop would pitch in, but who else? The race was scheduled for a Sunday afternoon. Smitty might be game. After a brief hesitation, John signed the form and handed it over. He had two weeks until the time trails; he would roust up some guys between now and then. The purse for this race was substantially more than Mercer's, with prize money awarded to the top four finishers. He could offer to pay his crew for their time. Imagine that, him paying Pop a salary for a change.

"We'll put an ad in the paper," Pop assured. "It will bring mechanics out of the woodwork. How much are you going to pay?"

"I don't know, maybe ten dollars. I'll only need them for a few hours."

"Count me in," Smitty hollered from under a sedan he was busy greasing. "I could use that ten dollars for my Christmas fund."

"See what I mean?" Pop said. "You could get by with the two of us, unless you want a bigger crew."

"That is, if you qualify," a familiar voice carried from just outside the bay door.

The men squinted to see the visitor walk out of the bright, sunlit afternoon and into the cool shade of the garage. It was Murphy, sporting his usual cigarette and tousled hair. Hadn't he ever heard of Brylcreem?

"Of course I'll qualify," John shot back.

Murphy sucked the breath through his teeth, pulled up an oil drum, and took a seat.

"I don't know. The boys at Heidelberg can be pretty tough. Mercer is a cakewalk. Oh, speaking of Mercer, congratulations on making the paper. I couldn't help but notice."

"Same to you," Pop casually replied for John. "Is there something we can help you with?"

Libbey, noticing the visitor, sauntered over and parked herself in front of Murphy. She had more than doubled her size in a few months and her face was no longer that of a puppy. Her neck was becoming thicker and she was beginning to take on a tough-looking demeanor.

Murphy stroked Libbey's head. She responded with a friendly lick of his hand.

"That's a good dog. Yes, actually, I need an alignment on the Ford. Usually do my own work, but I don't have the right equipment for an alignment. Can you get it done by Friday?"

"That should be fine." Out of habit, Pop removed his handkerchief and wiped his clean hands into it. "Come into the office and I'll write you up." Then, stopping himself, he said, "Wait, I'll let my new manager handle the paperwork."

John gave Pop a "thanks anyway" look and followed Murphy into the front office. Sunlight spilled through the full-length windows and the chairs popped with color like maraschino cherries atop a hot fudge sundae.

"You worked here a while?" Murphy questioned.

"I've been working for Pop on and off since I was ten."

"The old guy thinking of retiring, is that why he made you manager?"

"Pop's not going anywhere, and he's not that old. He's preparing more for my future than his."

"Ah." Murphy stood quietly while John wrote up his ticket. John felt uneasy. Something about Murphy didn't smell right. He acted and spoke friendly enough, but came off fake, as if he were trying to restrain something malicious that threatened to break through any moment. For the first time in his young life, John sensed what it must feel like to have an enemy, someone who would do harm if he could get away with it. Murphy was competitive. Any racer worth his salt should be competitive. There was more. Murphy was angry. John glanced up from his writing to see Murphy studying the back wall, his gaze moving across the room and resting on the door to the garage.

"Sign here, please."

Murphy penned his agreement to pay as billed upon completion and tossed his key on the counter.

"Take good care of her. I'm entrusting you with my machine—I'll know if anything is amiss."

John didn't know whether to be shocked or insulted. It never crossed his mind to tamper with Murphy's "machine." He smirked at the absurdity of it.

"You couldn't have brought her to a more honest shop."

"Oh, I know that. I know." Murphy nodded and pushed the front door open with enough force to make the bells clatter in protest.

Still and vacant, the track stretched flat before the rumbling coupe as John awaited the signal to begin his time trial. Dark clouds scuttled across the sky, threatening but holding back. John was in his favorite place, alone with his car and the empty strip before him, prepared to move as fast as his body, mind, and machine would allow. Performance was crucial to stay near the front of the lineup on race day, to hold an advantage toward a win.

The green flag shuttered and John sped off, taking her quickly to full throttle, riding inches from the short cement barrier at the curves, just at the edge of control. On the straight track, he shot a glance at the speedometer to see the needle shimmy up to ninety-eight miles per hour and knew he had it. Qualifying was not an issue. He kept a strong pace for a few laps, settling in at street speed, noticing the bleachers dotted here and there with spectators and the expanse of green field and trees beyond.

John pulled off the track as a newer model Ford slid into place for its turn on the round. One of the timekeepers strolled over to the coupe, squinting toward the darkening sky. John stood to greet him and offered his hand.

"Congratulations, you averaged sixty-three miles per hour. We clocked you at close to one hundred on the back straight." John smiled and nodded. "Check in tomorrow two hours before race time for your position, if this storm doesn't soak the track, that is."

Murphy had been right about one thing: competition at Heidelberg was stiff. John found himself fifteen places from the pole. Murphy sat six places back. John recognized several cars from the Mercer race, including the Mercury he fought with over second place and the black "eight ball" Buick. A conglomeration of machinery in all shapes and colors huddled at the starting line, drivers at the ready.

The track was still moist, saturated the night before by the storm that finally let loose, but had sucked up enough of the water to be race ready. Second place would be a stretch this time, but he was determined to try.

The call to start engines was given; the rumble of metal coming to life rose on the thick air. To John, the sound was sweeter than a symphony tuning to the concertmaster's guiding note before a performance. He fastened his helmet strap and gripped the steering wheel, foot pressed against the brake to hold his charger ready. The flag signaled the pace car to begin its lap as the huddle of cars followed, gradually picking up speed around the first lap, gaining empty space between them. John noticed the track felt a bit "thick" due to the wetness of the earth. The pace car, a white convertible sedan, left the track and let the boys run free.

The coupe ran strong and tight. John entered the zone quickly, slipping past one car after another. He planned his strategy one car at a time, riding close on the next target's bumper to unnerve the driver, finessing around to present and, when the timing was precise, slipping ahead with a surge of just enough speed to get where he needed to be: in front of the target. He rode up and down the track as traffic would allow, avoiding being passed himself. In the span of thirty-two laps, he had gained seventh position. He held there for ten more laps. With each advance, it became more challenging to pass the next driver. A Buick skid out of control and lost a tire. The black rubber doughnut bounded across the track, cars swerving around the rolling debris until it finally came to rest in the grassy center. The incident broke John's concentration as he slowed and veered around the tire, avoiding a collision with other cars in the process. Whoever thought stock racing was simply driving around in circles never tried it. Track conditions and speed tortured the cars, ripping tires from their axles, sending cars reeling out of control all within mere inches of each other and the wall that contained the chaos. The clear track could become an instantaneous obstacle course. A guy had to be on the ball to keep control.

There was not time to bring out the yellow flag before the race returned to full intensity. John struggled for over twenty laps before finally taking sixth place from an Olds. He and the coupe soared around the track; he never felt so free and yet utterly in control.

"Just two more for the gold, two for the gold," John confirmed to himself in an effort to keep pushing. Fourth place or higher won cash, and he needed to win. For this race, there was an obligation of payment to his pit crew. A rush of adrenaline followed the realization that he was within reach. Fifth place eluded him for an eternity. He traded places with a Chrysler that just wouldn't let up three times in the space of fifty laps. The slogan "Watch the Fords go by!" rang in John's head the third time he passed the Chrysler, and this time he meant it. Mashing the accelerator, he held fifth place for ten laps then daringly approached fourth. Did he need gas? Too intense to check, John kept going. Fourth place was where the money was, and right where Murphy's big, black Ford was holding.

John stopped breathing. It was happening. The coupe slowly gained on Murphy's Ford, inching ahead on the outside, ready to slip down in front of the black '02. *Hold on, keep focus.* John groaned as the engine strained at full throttle. For an instant, there were only two cars on the track: the black Ford in fourth place, a mass of foreboding power, and the little, white coupe with the speed and agility to take on anything.

The two approached the third curve; they would have to slow to make the turn. John would use the curve to his advantage, taking it as fast as possible to stay ahead of Murphy, riding the outside and then cutting down in front. There was the opening—Murphy had a good two car lengths in front of him before the next contender. The curve came up fast, too fast. The black Ford moved closer to the coupe, rising up the bank. In an instant, John heard the clunk of metal, felt the impact as the Ford smacked his rear fender. The impact sent the coupe's back end screeching toward the cement wall as her tires let go of what little hold they had on the dirt. John felt the muscles in his arms bulging, straining to control the wheel. Instinctively his foot went to the brake to reduce the coupe's speed, now sliding sideways along the track.

"No! Damn it!" John cried out as he fought to point the coupe forward. He had moved into the center of the track now as cars screeched and slid around him. *Bam!* Another driver plowed into his rear fender, sending the coupe spinning. All control was lost. Through the windshield, John saw the earth come up to kiss the windshield, felt the seatbelt dig into his pelvis and the steering wheel wrench from his grasp as the coupe flipped twice then stopped with a bang, the front end perched on the chain-link fence that separated the track from the spectator area along the front straightaway.

John hurriedly studied his position. The front right tire was at least two feet off the ground; there was no point in trying to get back in the race. He was done. He turned off the engine. John felt lightheaded and as if he would retch. Up ahead he glimpsed the yellow flag positioned over the track. The pace car had come out and was guiding the slowed racers around the track. John saw concerned glances from drivers as they passed the coupe, a quick turn of the head or wave of the hand to wish him well as they danced around the wreckage.

His knees shook and his heart jumped like a jackhammer. He released the leather strap from the coupe's door—thank God, it was there—and made his exit.

He saw Pop running toward him along the outside of the fence in the spectator area. He must have crossed the track from pit row. A loud cheer and applause rose from the bleachers as John stood outside the coupe and removed his helmet, sprinting toward the opening that would take him off the track. A tow truck rolled up to the coupe. Pop met him at the entrance and wrapped his arm protectively around John's shoulders.

"I'm all right. I'm all right," John responded, a tone of disgust in his voice.

The two men silently watched the crew lift John's baby off the fence and wheel her past the finish line and toward the gate.

"Nothing we can't fix," Pop assured. He gave John's shoulder a reassuring squeeze and padded after the tow truck to assess the damage.

John's heart had stopped knocking against his rib cage, but his knees were still shaking under his trousers. He watched as his partner, dirt smeared and battered, was slowly towed off trackside. All he could do was follow behind her as the remaining racers roared back to full speed.

He stopped for a few moments to watch the action, standing alongside the grandstand. The constant throng of engines zoomed past, glistening chrome and polished yet dusty metal whizzing by. He ached to be there and not stranded, watching from the sidelines. He noticed Murphy was still in, running fourth place. It figured. John felt sure Murphy had clipped him on purpose. He knew Murphy's level of skill and that he could have made the turn without inching close enough to hit the coupe. Now it was more than competition. It was war.

The clamor of spectators rose behind him, as if a switch in his brain had suddenly tuned to their wavelength. John turned to scan the crowd; the cheering, jeering swell of humanity crammed together, eyes fixated as one being on the track. Except for one person, just a few rows up, who was looking his way. John centered his gaze and focused on the sole admirer. It was Maggie. She sat quietly, one hand resting in her lap and the other placed on the knee of a man in dress shirt and tie, sleeves rolled up to ease the midday heat; he was intently studying the track. *Must be Bob,* John reasoned. Bob cupped his hands around his mouth and hollered over the deafening roar, "Get a move on, 19! I've got fifty bucks on you."

Maggie gave a little shrug and smile toward John, a sad smile that said she understood his plight. John realized she had seen the whole thing: his roll and hang-up on the fence. Of the thousands of spectators at the track that day, she was probably the only one genuinely concerned when that happened. Had she told Bob that she knew the driver in 23, had visited this track with him one chilly spring night and touched the white car that was now racing around the track? With her free hand, she turned toward John and blew him a kiss, silent and soft, unseen among the hundreds of eyes surrounding them.

John lifted his hand and caught his prize, tucking it neatly in his shirt pocket, patting it gently and returning his biggest smile. Maggie smiled back then turned her head quickly to respond to a comment from Bob who was obviously unaware of John's presence. John looked away and walked quickly off the field.

Chapter Eight

Bologna again. Only two weeks into the school year, and John was already sick of bologna sandwiches with mustard on white. If only Momma would let him pack his own lunch, but she was determined to do it. He washed down a mouthful of bread with a swig of milk and moved on to a more palatable offering: Momma's apple bread. Thick, moist, and sweet; her home-baked treats made the day more bearable. Not that John disliked high school. He was smart and had no problem pulling good grades. Much of it seemed a waste of his time. He was still paying for repairs from the Heidelberg accident and working extra hours at the shop on weekends. If not for school, he would be able to work full time.

John usually sat alone for lunch, on the periphery of conversation and only offering occasional input, while the other guys horsed around and bragged about the girl they dated last weekend or their last great play on the football field. This day was not unlike any other, except when John crumpled his last paper wrapper and stood up from the hard cafeteria bench, he was surrounded by three guys he had not noticed before.

"So, you're a racecar driver," one of them started.

"Yeah, I ran a few races this summer."

"We saw you in the paper after the Mercer run. Is that your own car?"

"Yep." John wondered what they wanted.

"A few of us belong to a car club that meets in my dad's garage. It's pretty exclusive, only guys who really know cars can join. We're rebuilding a '32 Ford, wondered if you'd like to join us. The club meets twice a week after school and on Saturdays."

The three young men looked eagerly at John, hoping for a yes.

"I'll have to think on it. I work after school, and after graduation, I'll be pretty busy with the race circuit and keeping the coupe in top form." How else could he politely tell them that work on any car other than his own, unless getting paid for it, was not an effective use of his time?

"Sure, sure," the leader nodded. "How about I give you my phone number and you call me if you change your mind." With no one having any loose paper, John handed over his American history text and watched his new acquaintance pencil on the back page "Mark, the Road Knights" and his number. "Come by sometime. Even if you can't join, we'll make you an honorary member."

Mark's two associates nodded in agreement.

"Thanks, Mark." John extended his hand.

"Anytime, Powerhouse."

John beamed at hearing his pet name.

Road Knights. Not a bad name. That was precisely what he became out there on the track, the car his suit of armor, jousting to win the prize of prestige, of money, and because it was exciting as hell. There was even a pretty maiden at the finish to offer a kiss. John smirked at the simile—amazing he hadn't thought of it before. These "knights" would most likely supe up their '32 just enough to beat some competing group of grease monkeys in a road race. The chances of him seeing Mark on the racetrack were slim to none.

John strode along the polished narrow corridor toward his history class feeling pretty smug. He had already known support, training, financial means to pursue his dream of racing for several years where others were just beginning to dabble. For the first time, John realized what an advantage his relationship with Pop and his job at the garage had given him. He had every means to succeed.

Perhaps it was John's upbeat mood and general sense of cockiness after meeting the Road Knights that made him finally take notice of Helen Grant. Sitting in the back row next to the window, tapping her pencil on the desk in boredom waiting for class to start, Helen's lovely face caught John's attention. While students entered and took their seats, John lingered at the doorway, staring until he caught her eye. John flashed his best smile and held eye contact. Helen snapped to attention and smiled back, holding his gaze in her blue eyes like a cup of cool water. John pointed to his watch and then the door, signaling that she should meet him after class. She nodded quickly and then looked around to see if anyone had noticed. No one had. The bell shrilled a warning to get down to business as John took his customary front row seat.

"Do you remember me, Helen?"

"Of course! You're John Powers. We met at the garage where Daddy takes his car. Do you still have that precious little dog?"

"Still have her, but she's getting bigger. Have you ever seen a Rottweiler full grown?"

"Can't say that I have."

The two walked slowly among the hustle of students rushing to grab books from their lockers or to reach their next class. John glanced at his watch; they still had five minutes. "Would you like to meet me at the diner after school for a Coke or something?"

Helen stopped and smiled up at John. Her neck and face flushed pink against her crisp, white, cotton blouse. John liked how perfectly her dark eyebrows arched and the redness of her lips.

"I'd love to, John, but I have choir practice right after sixth period. How about tomorrow?" That worked too. "Okay, then. I'll see you tomorrow."

That was easy, thought John as he watched Helen stride off to her next class. His eyes followed up and down, from her dark, pageboy hairstyle down to her penny loafers, stopping along the way to admire the young figure in between. He knew she had liked him from the first time they met. She was pretty enough, just his age, and most importantly, not married to a traveling salesman.

"Hold still. Perfect." The bulb flashed with a *pop* and left blue circles floating in the air. Dad quickly swirled the clouded bulb from the camera's silver flash bowl and replaced it with a fresh one. "Just one more." John and Helen stood poised and smiling, Momma and Susan admiring the pair from the sofa. Helen stood eye level with John in her stilettos; pale-pink fabric swished over crinoline when she moved. The two had endured the first photo shoot at Helen's house. Now they waited for Pop to arrive with his Olds so John could borrow his ride for the night. Even though the race damage from the prior summer had been mended, Momma wouldn't hear of John taking Helen to the prom in the coupe, and Dad's Ford was, well, not up to the occasion.

"Helen looks pretty!" Susan exclaimed from her seat on the couch. The evening sun spilled through the front window, splashing across Helen's salmon-pink dress and lighting up her sparkling blue eyes.

"Yes, doesn't she?" Momma almost cooed. Marilyn Powers loved Helen. Within a week of John and Helen's first date, she had insisted Helen join the family once a week for dinner with John driving her home after each visit. Every Wednesday, John would forgo working at the garage after school to please his mother and spend time with Helen. He didn't mind; it was actually a nice break. Momma was sunnier on those Wednesdays, greeting them at the door while wearing one of her best dresses and heels and donning lipstick. Momma busied herself in the kitchen or reposed on the sofa while twisting yarn around knitting needles so she could create shawls to sell at the next church bazaar. Helen and John would sit silently at the table and work on homework or study for an upcoming exam. Just before his Father arrived from work, John would stay out of the way as his mother and Helen set the table and talked about the latest sale at Macy's or what type of dessert went best with pot roast. Susan stood by as Helen helped Momma in the kitchen, absorbing everything about Helen she could: her way of speaking, her mannerisms, and her laugh. Susan could not get enough of this "pretty girl" who joined their family once a week. John knew Helen filled a hole in Momma's heart that no one else could.

Now the school year was almost over and both would be graduating. Helen's father wanted her to enter college in the fall, and she had been accepted by two universities out of state—one of them Radcliffe. John knew that once Helen tasted college life, had seen the world outside Pittsburg, he would probably never see her again. John would miss her, but he was more worried about how Momma would get by. Perhaps that was why he had not told his parents about Helen's college plans yet.

"She's all cleaned up and ready!" Pop hollered as he walked through the front door.

Momma jumped from her seat. "Heavens, I almost forgot about dinner."

"Let me help," Helen offered.

"No, I won't hear of it. This is your special night! Do you want to spill something on that gorgeous dress?"

Pop tossed the keys to John who snatched them out of midair and started for the door.

"Aren't you forgetting something?" his father said. John looked puzzled, until Momma came from the kitchen with a boxed corsage retrieved from the fridge. Dad gave his son a critical look. That was nothing new; John had received many such looks in the last year. While he never said anything directly against John's favorite pastime, Dad did not offer any support. John knew his father was not in favor of his racing and thought he should pursue higher goals than working at the garage after high school. His father saw stock-car racing as a reckless waste of time and money. The sport was all right for other people, not for his son.

Dad's displeasure slowly spilled over into criticism about John's character and mannerisms, his sarcasm and negative comments making it difficult for John to spend any time with his father without feeling inadequate. When he wasn't subtly cutting John down with his words, Dad's looks said, "Grow up and start thinking about your future." What he didn't know was that John had been doing just that. Too bad his father couldn't follow him at school and see how the other guys respected him, almost to the point of being intimidated, due to his reputation on the track.

John pinned the spray of white tea rosebuds on Helen's bodice and noticed the pink ribbon matched the shade of her dress. That must be why Momma asked her to bring the dress by last week—so she could order the perfect shade of ribbon. Women cared about that sort of thing. He never would have thought it mattered.

John took Helen's hand and headed toward the door. Momma ran over and gave each a kiss. Oh, jeez, she was tearing up.

"You two have a wonderful time, and drive safely."

John grinned at his mother. "Actually," he responded, "I thought I'd take a few turns around the track on the way to the dance."

Pop chuckled.

"Don't be a smart-ass," Dad replied. "She was just using an expression."

John lost his smile and nodded in his father's direction before escorting Helen to the car.

"Your mom is so sweet," Helen said as she slid into the passenger seat.

"Yep, I don't know where we'd be without her."

Chapter Nine

MOMMA'S SHADOWED SILHOUETTE RESTED dark against the pale slivers of light that slipped casually through the vertical blinds. Her profile worn and defeated, wisps of hair loosened from her neat updo, framing her forehead and the back of her neck. The room was dark and quiet save for the whisper of shallow breathing from the bed, a stark contrast to the brightness of the hallway just outside the door where John stood peering in.

His eyes adjusted after a few moments to let in muted color and shape, enough to see Momma caressing the hand of her sick little girl between her own. Susan lay still and small beneath the thin, blue blanket, her face buried under an oxygen mask. John wanted to rip the mask from her face, lift her in his arms, and run—run out into the afternoon sunshine, into a place of life and happiness. Instead, he stepped quietly into the room and sat in the chair adjacent to Susan's bed. Momma slowly looked up, her face expressionless.

"Dad's parking the car," John offered.

Momma nodded, silent tears moistening her cheeks, and stroked Susan's soft hair with her fingertips.

Seeing Susan like this was almost unbearable. This place felt surreal, like a strange dream from which he couldn't wake up. He knew Momma had called them to the hospital to say good-bye. "Come right away," she had weakly cried into the phone. Susan's pneumonia had worsened during the night. Doctors had drained fluid from her lungs, but it continued to form. She had not responded to treatment; they didn't know what else to do for her.

John stared down at his sister, willing life and energy into her body, praying for strength to beat this illness that had started as a mild bronchial infection and slowly worsened to a deep, hoarse cough that would not recede despite the doctor's care. Only three nights ago, when the coughing brought up white foam and her breath rattled in her chest, Dad had scooped her feverish body from her purple bed, blankets and all, bundled her in the back of the Ford, and driven her to the hospital. There she had stayed and had grown weaker. The oxygen tank hissed in John's ear. Why wasn't it working? Why did nothing work? How could God let this happen to Susan? Hadn't she suffered enough? How could He do this to Momma? Sporadic thoughts tumbled in John's mind as he sat in the darkened room. Darkness was apropos; they were losing the light of Susan's life, and no one wanted to flip the switch to view the glaring truth. It would have been disrespectful, shameful somehow, to shine a bright light on such sorrow.

The distant tap of Dad's footfalls along the hospital corridor approached, quick and determined. John's eyes glanced to the small table next to Susan's bed where her gray-rimmed glasses stared back at him. He picked them up, slipping them into his shirt pocket. Dad appeared at the door and stood for a moment as John had done, taking in the scene before him. Momma turned to look at her husband, so strong and yet so helpless, and began to cry harder. Dad entered the room and leaned over his wife, wrapping his arms around her shoulders, pressing his face against hers, slowly rocking, rocking back and forth as she sobbed, quietly sharing in her pain.

"I know, I know."

John felt a lump rise to his throat at the tenderness shared between his parents in this awful moment. His presence in the room seemed awkward and uncomfortable. The dim walls closed in around him. He quietly rose and walked into the hallway, down the corridor, and to the reception area.

He sat in the brightness and stared at a pile of magazines placed there to serve as a diversion for those waiting upon providence. He picked up a *National Geographic* and flipped through its pages. Bright colors jumped at him yet triggered no response; stories that would normally have piqued his interest sat as only blurs of black dots on white backdrops.

A row of black chairs sat across from him, all unoccupied save for at the far end where a man sat quietly reading a story to a little girl snuggled on his lap. The girl, all of three years old, leaned against her father's chest and shyly glanced between pictures of the Pokey Little Puppy and John. She smiled at him, her eyes flirting, as her father cajoled her to pay attention to the story. John glanced back and gave a little smile.

The child giggled and waved in response. "Hi!" Her little voice was full of excitement. Her presence was too much for John, who rested his head in his hands and began to cry. He struggled to choke the sobs that threatened to break from his throat, to hide his face from the little girl so as not to frighten her.

A small voice penetrated his sorrow. "Why is that man sad, Daddy?"

Her father whispered his reply. "I don't know, honey." Then, a moment later, he said, "Perhaps we should say a silent prayer so he won't be sad anymore."

"Okay," the child whispered.

The room fell painfully quiet as John recuperated. He could not look in their direction lest he break down again. Instead, he glared down at the coffee table strewn with magazines.

"Amen," came the little voice. Then the story of the pokey little puppy resumed until the girl's mother came to fetch the pair.

The man lingered a moment as his family left the waiting room, approaching slowly until John looked up at him. He rested a warm hand on John's shoulder as he walked past. "God bless you, son."

"Yes. Thank you." John nodded. He watched the family leave, feeling embarrassed at his display of emotion yet thankful for the man's response. Some people were truly kind.

Over an hour later, John wondered if he should head back to Susan's room. No one had come for him. Perhaps his parents wanted to be alone with her a while longer. The afternoon had turned to evening. He would return and ask his parents for some time alone with her. Maybe she was awake now.

Upon reaching the doorway to Susan's room, John was surprised to find it empty, the sheets and blanket bunched at the foot of the bed. John felt disoriented and checked the room number again. Yes, this was it. He began to panic and ran toward the nurses' station.

"Susan Powers ... Susan, where is she?" he stammered.

The white-capped nurse rose from her seat behind the counter and quickly came around to take John's arm. "Your parents are with the doctor; he can explain." She led him in the opposite direction of the waiting area, down the corridor and then another, stopping at the attending physician's office door.

The doctor sat behind a desk of dark mahogany framed by a window full of purpled twilight. He saw John at the doorway and immediately arose. John's parents turned to look at him and he knew, could tell by his father's red and swollen eyes and the whiteness of his mother's face, that Susan was gone.

"Ah, here you are," the doctor said as he extended a hand to John. "We were just about to come find you." His voice was soothing and deep. "Have a seat. John, is it?" John's body obeyed and fell into the soft chair behind the desk, yet his mind felt sluggish, as if he were asleep.

The doctor's voice was slow and far away as John heard how Susan's body could no longer fight, how she had not responded to the antibiotics given to her over the past several days, how her lungs collapsed and their attempts to revive her were unsuccessful. The doctor perched on the corner of his desk when he spoke, looking directly in John's face, yet it was difficult for John to understand his words. His white coat filled John's range of vision as the doctor rose and walked to the door. "I'll leave you folks alone for a little while. Please stay as long as you need to."

John looked blankly at his parents seated across the desk. There were no words; he could think of nothing to say. Anger swelled inside as he sat in the silence. Why had they not come for him? He didn't even have a chance to say good-bye. He felt cheated.

His mother must have sensed his thoughts and was the first to speak. "Oh, John, we didn't know where you had gone and it happened so quickly! Suddenly the room was full of people and the doctor came in; we couldn't leave Susan's side to come find you."

Yes, it made sense, but it didn't hurt any less, didn't squelch the anger that made his eyes sting with tears and his breath catch in his chest.

"You had been gone for quite a while when it happened," his father spoke now. "We had just said one of us should go find you and then decided you would come back soon. Then Susan stopped breathing and we called for the nurse. She was incoherent, unresponsive." Dad waved his hand as if pushing the matter aside. "She wouldn't have known you were there. You'll just have to remember her how she was."

His father looked down at the floor, refusing to make eye contact. The matter was closed.

John was not ready for it to be closed; he had wanted to see his sister alone before she died, to tell her how much she meant to him. Even if she couldn't respond, he knew she would have heard and understood. He was closer to her than anyone else, understood her better than even Momma. He was her Johnny. It was important to him. Couldn't anyone understand that?

His father's dismissal of the issue only made him angrier. He closed his eyes to shut down the feelings, to stuff them reprehensively inside in a deep place where only he could go to pull them up and mill over them at will like a dark stone fished from the bottom of a river. He did it quickly to avoid saying what he really thought, from lashing out and perhaps causing irreparable damage. He loved Susan, had built a childhood of memories with her, yet he didn't matter. It was not important enough to come find him when she was dying, even though he was just down the corridor. No one had even tried. He clenched his fists so hard his nails bit into his palms.

The little girl's prayer hadn't worked. John's heart was breaking.

Chapter Ten

SUMMER OF 1952 IN Pittsburg was hot enough to melt the tar on Highway 837. Though it was early September, the heat lingered. This night there was no breeze to toss the air, and it hung thick and heavy over the drive-in theater where John and Helen sat in the coupe while blankly staring at the glowing screen. Gary Cooper was preparing to meet the town nemesis at high noon. Typically, they would be all over each other by intermission. Helen was in her "don't touch me" mood tonight, and John assumed she must be experiencing "that time of the month." John and Helen had discovered sex and enjoyed embarking every chance they could. Of course, there was the initial cajoling by John and the promise that, yes, of course he planned to marry her, before Helen would move past necking. After all, she was leaving for Radcliffe in a few weeks. They might as well enjoy each other while they could.

As neither set of parents ever went out in the evening, that left the back of the coupe as the most viable spot. John often wished he had opted for a sedan, a family model with more room. But the coupe was fast and easy to handle in the track, and that's what really mattered. He was having quite a summer, racing the local circuit and making a reputation for himself as an aggressive young driver who would do whatever it took to win. The white coupe with its 23 emblazoned on each door had become a local attraction, with honks and cheers filling the drive-in when he and Helen pulled in. He would arrive just minutes before the show, when the lot was most full, and drive around the perimeter to get the full effect.

Intermission arrived with its cartoon soda pop, popcorn, and hotdog parade marching across the screen. "Do you want anything?" John asked.

Helen shook her head. "John, we have to talk." Her tone was somber.

"Sure. What's wrong?"

Helen twisted her hands in her lap and struggled to make eye contact.

"Can we go somewhere else? I don't want to talk here."

John replaced the speaker on its perch and started up the coupe, slowly rolling over the graveled lot and outside the drive-in theater.

"Do you want me to take you home?" Helen shook her head. "How about the park? It's a clear night." Helen smiled and nodded.

They drove in silence to Grandview Park, just south of the river across from which sat Pittsburgh's golden triangle. John had presumed Helen might break off their relationship before leaving for college; that must be what she wanted to talk about. She was intelligent and had the support of her father's money to pursue whatever she wanted. Why would she stay in Pittsburgh with a shop mechanic and part-time stock-car racer? While the thought of losing Helen saddened John, he had been bracing himself for it since before graduation. He had plenty to keep him busy and would have no trouble meeting other pretty girls. They had come out in droves to the racetrack, screaming his name when he pulled into position before the race and again when he had made it to victory lane. No, there would be no shortage of female companionship in John's life.

He parked the coupe and the pair found a bench looking toward the Monongahela River. It brought to mind a similar evening when John and Maggie had stood sharing their aspirations. He wondered how Maggie was faring, if she had saved enough to open her boutique.

Helen released a long sigh and turned to face John. "I'm just going to say it because it will be easier. Johnny, I'm pregnant."

There was no response at first, just a blank stare, so Helen repeated herself. "Pregnant."

"Ohhh." He hadn't expected this. "How long?"

"Only recently. I'm due in May." John was startled but didn't want to upset Helen. He took her hand in his and gave a soft squeeze as he tried to get his head around the fact that he was going to be a father at the age of eighteen.

"That's *g-g-great* news," he stammered.

"Is it?" Helen retorted.

"Well, yes! You're going to have our baby. That's good news."

"Not according to my parents."

"You told them?"

"I had to; Mother was getting suspicious and finally took me to the doctor. Daddy says I have to get rid of it if I want to go to college."

John felt queasy.

"Get rid of it … You mean an abortion?" Helen nodded, her eyes filling with tears.

"Daddy has a friend, another doctor, who will do it through the first trimester."

"What do you want to do?"

"Oh, I don't know," Helen said. "I've wanted to go to Radcliffe so badly, but not if it means killing my baby, probably never seeing you again. I've always wanted to be a mother, and I love you, John. I love being with you. College will always be there for later."

John wrapped his arms around Helen's shoulders and rested his head on hers. They sat for a long while, staring out toward the lights of Pittsburg shimmering in the blackness. His heart was pounding almost as intensely as during a race, when his whole body was given over to concentration on a single goal. He felt shocked and angry that someone would suggest they "get rid of" his baby. Like hell. He would show them how well he could take care of things.

As he sat quietly with Helen and mulled over the situation, his anger slowly gave way to a mild sense of panic. This changed everything. He would have to support a wife and kid while pursing his racing career.

There were other drivers who did it, bringing their family to the track on race day or simply leaving them home when on the traveling circuit. He did have a steady job with Pop and would continue to have access to what he needed for the coupe wholesale. He had planned to move from his parents' home in the next year anyway. How much more could it cost? This just provided the incentive to move forward with his plans. But was he really ready to marry Helen? He had casually mentioned it as something that would happen "out there" in the future, after she returned from college. He half expected that she would lose interest in him, leaving him to pursue his true desire, which was racing the NASCAR circuit. He had never felt overtly romantic toward her, but he wasn't sure he could feel that way about anyone. Helen was certainly accomplished and easy to look at, and she would do anything for him. As long as she didn't interfere with his racing career, what else did he need?

"Helen, why don't we get married? Right away. I'd planned to rent my own place soon, and …"

Helen put her fingers to his lips to silence them and then gave him a gentle kiss. "Tell me you're not asking me to marry you just because of the baby." John began to protest. "Tell me!"

"I'm not marrying you just because of the baby," John answered slowly and deliberately. His eyes assured that he meant every word, but his gut hadn't gotten the message.

"You're Patrick Powers's boy." The day-shift supervisor invited John into his office. Despite the heat in the mill, John shivered at the sterile, green tile, metal desk, and dirty, white walls. The supervisor picked up a manila folder and opened it across his desk. "I've reviewed your application. If you're anything like your father, you have a good work ethic."

"Yes, sir." The supervisor sat across a soiled and worn desk, from years of use just outside the steel mill floor, and stared at John with puffy, expressionless eyes.

"Tell me, aside from your father's position as senior foreman, why are you seeking employment at US Steel?"

John shifted in his chair and prepared to spew his rehearsed line. "Well, I've recently married and am looking for a steady position to support my new family." No sense going on about wanting to work in the steel business, career development, and the like. It would have been all lies. John couldn't care less about a future with the mill. It was just temporary until he could get into the national racing circuit and make some real money.

"Ah." The man leaned back in his swivel chair and glanced at John's paperwork. "It says here that you plan to work evenings at a garage, is that right?"

John felt as if he were on trial. "Yes, I've worked for Pop for many years, but he is unable to pay enough to—" John stopped himself. He was not accustomed to being vague and couldn't deal with it now. He leaned forward and rested his arms on the oily desk. "Look," he began, "I need this job. We have a baby on the way and I need more money and a job that offers benefits."

"That is commendable." The supervisor leaned forward now, his face limp and pale as the walls. "But we don't take well to moonlighting here. We need our employees to be sharp, on the ball. Also, you should know that our benefit package doesn't cover maternity, only illness."

Great, John thought. Something else he would have to pay for. Perhaps Dr. Grant would offer them a family discount. Still, he needed to turn this around and convince Mr. Paleface that he should hire him.

"Oh, that wouldn't be a problem," John retorted. "I've worked for Pop while going to school as long as I can remember, and you can see there I was able to keep my grades up. It would only be a few hours, just a couple nights a week to supplement my income. He's a long-time friend of the family and I don't want to leave him in the lurch." That was partially true. Now that Pop had hired a third mechanic to help him and Smitty and had resumed his role managing the shop, John's services were needed but not crucial. John planned to work for Pop immediately after leaving the mill at 3:00 until beyond closing, working on the coupe after hours as needed. Pop had already agreed to his arrangement; John would have free use of the shop and access to parts, tires, and maintenance items for the coupe in lieu of a salary. Further, he could take off for time trials and races that happened to fall on weeknights or Saturdays. He desperately needed to maintain his relationship with Pop's wholesale connections. Pure Oil had just released a new tire designed specifically for stock racing that he had to get his hands on. He also planned to supercharge the engine over the winter.

John had made sure not to mention his racing plans on the mill application. It was none of their business what he did in his own time.

The supervisor hesitated and looked once again at John's application. "Well, I don't think it will be a problem. We have a few employees taking correspondence courses in the evening—it's not much different than that, is it?" His eyes actually brightened slightly as he flashed a strained smile at John. "Besides, you're the son of a long-term employee, and that certainly stands for something. We have a day-shift position open on the hot saw. Show up here Monday at 7:00 and it's yours."

John gave a relieved laugh and stood to shake his new boss's hand. "Thank you. You won't be disappointed."

Only a few more days of freedom until he would be bound to the stifling, sweat-rendering heat and noise of the steel mill, would be coming home with the same smell in his nostrils that permeated his father's clothes and filled the front hall until he shuffled upstairs and into the shower. It felt like he was sentenced to time in prison with the chance of escape for a few waking hours each day.

John climbed the cement steps leading to his rented bungalow. He had been fortunate to find such a spacious home to rent, complete with two bedrooms and a garage. The widow who let it go could no longer handle the upkeep and moved to Florida to live with her sister. John's salary made the place out of reach. He negotiated the rent with the promise to replace the roof by spring.

Despite the garage, the coupe was not parked there; number 23 lived at the shop. Dr. Grant had made it clear that his daughter would not be seen driving around town in a racecar with John "Powerhouse" Powers emblazoned over the door. He had purchased a slightly used Buick as the couple's wedding gift, with the comment that since Helen was blowing off college he had some extra cash to spend on their wedding.

"Did you get it?" Helen emerged from the back of the house while drying her hands on her apron.

"Start Monday," John replied, lifting Helen by the waist and spinning her around right there in the hallway. She laughed with delight.

"Now we can pay the rent on time. Oh, John, I'm so relieved! How long until your first paycheck?" Helen started back toward the kitchen.

"Don't know. I didn't ask. Say, you are starting to grow." John approached Helen from behind and rested one hand on her firm belly while wrapping his other arm around her shoulders. She stopped and relaxed into his body.

"Momma says it's a boy due to how bad my morning sickness was." She turned and looked at her husband. "You would probably rather have a son, someone to crawl under a chassis with, who can help you take a car apart and put it back together."

"Oh, I dunno. It would be fun having a little girl to spoil rotten, just like her mother."

"I am not spoiled!" Helen objected. "Look at me, slaving away in the kitchen making an apple pie to take to your folks for dinner tonight, and I have to get it in the oven or we'll be late. Your father is going to be so proud when he hears about your job at the mill."

"Yes, that should keep him quiet for a while, at least until next spring."

Helen brushed the raw piecrust with milk, sprinkled it with sugar, and slid it into the heated oven.

"Why? What happens next spring?"

"I told you, don't you remember? The Midwest Association for Racecars' new car tour starts in May, and I plan to be part of it. I'll never make it to NASCAR sticking with the local tracks."

Helen removed her apron and slowly and neatly folded it, her demeanor becoming serious and guarded. "*New* car tour? But you don't have a new car."

"That's right. I plan to buy one. Pop has connections at most of the dealerships in town; I should get a sweet deal on a …"

"But the baby is due in May."

"I know that. It's not as if I'll be that far away: Dayton, Ohio, Detroit, even right here in Pennsylvania. Besides, I'll come home in between races when I can. Your mother is here to help you with the baby. I'd just be in the way anyhow."

Helen was persistent. "What about your job at the mill? They won't give you all summer off to travel around the country and race."

John became defensive. "Forget the mill! That's not what I plan to do with my life, Helen, work in some stifling, stinking factory job like my old man and have the life sucked out of me."

Helen shot back. "But we need the money! Now you're going to throw away what little we have on a new racecar. How do you expect us to get by if you lose your job so you can chase after your hobby?"

"This isn't a hobby, it's what I do. It's who I am, and you're going to have to deal with that. You've known that since high school. Why should it be different now?"

"Oh, I don't know," Helen replied with angered sarcasm. "I thought maybe becoming a father would make you grow up."

"Hey, it takes a real man to step out of the mold and do what he really wants to do. I've known what I've wanted since I was ten, and I'm not giving it up for you or anyone else."

Helen slumped into the dinette chair, her face ashen. "I'm not trying to hold you back," she quietly said, "but you have to realize you have responsibilities. We can't always have things the way we want them. Do you think I wanted to give up college? Sometimes you have to make sacrifices to do the right thing."

"Oh, God, are you going to throw the college thing up to me for the rest of my life?"

Helen reached across the table to where John stood and grabbed his hand. John snatched it away.

"No, I don't mean to throw anything up to you. That was my decision. I feel it was the right decision, but I need to know you're going to hold up your end of the bargain."

"And what is that? To give up my dreams so you can feel comfortable? I'd end up resenting you the rest of my life. No, this is the right thing. I'm going to pursue it with everything I have."

Helen looked away. "Fine, if that's what you really want. I'm not going to stop you." She rose and opened the oven door, more as an excuse to exit the conversation than to check on the pie. The scent of warm apples and cinnamon wafted through the kitchen.

"You have nothing to worry about," John assured. "I'll make so much money racing you'll thank the day I walked away from the steel mill."

Helen leaned against the kitchen counter, her arms tightly crossed. "I hope you're right."

John pulled the creased and soiled slip of paper from his wallet and laid it on the counter. The pencil was smudged a bit, but he could still read the number he had torn from his history text: "Mark, the Road Knights."

A woman answered the phone. "Mark is working right now. He'll be home at seven; can I have him call you?"

"No, thanks. Where is he working these days?"

"Who is this, please?"

"John. John Powers. I'm a friend from high school."

"He's stock manager at the A&P. He's usually home by now. They have him working late."

John thanked Mark's mother for the information and grabbed his coat. Libbey strode up, anxious for a walk, and nuzzled his hand. "Not right now, girl." John stroked her slick black fur. He opened the shop door and hollered to Pop over the noise of an air compressor. "I have to run out for a while, should be back within the hour."

Pop nodded an acknowledgment while loosening lug nuts from a dairy truck.

Brisk January air bit at his face as John walked the few blocks to the A&P. He never remembered to wear the scarf Momma had given him for Christmas until it was too late. Hand-knit of thick wool, it would have helped now. Only a few cars sat in front of the grocery. It was dinnertime and most folks were at home around the table. John usually took dinner late, wolfing down whatever Helen could reheat when he finally made it home. He often read the paper while Helen warmed his food, usually meatloaf or a casserole of whatever leftovers she had on hand. Most nights John barely made it past dinner before falling into bed, exhausted, only to get up at 5:30 the next morning to percolate some coffee, grab his lunch, and head to the mill. When that job was done for the day, he would peel off his asbestos suit, rush home, shower, and leave again for the shop.

John walked quickly through the store, peering down each aisle. There was no sight of Mark, so he decided to ask the cashier for help.

"He's back in the office." Then, over the intercom, she announced, "Mark, you're wanted upfront."

John wondered if Mark would remember him. They hadn't spoken since that fall day over a year ago. He saw Mark approaching from the produce aisle, a pencil tucked behind his ear.

"Hey ya, Powerhouse!" Mark remembered him. "What brings you to the A&P? You know, we don't sell any motor oil here." Mark laughed at his own cleverness. He had youthful energy, too much energy, John thought, to be cooped up in a back office at A&P.

"I found your number and your mom said you were working late tonight. Listen, are you still interested in cars?"

"Sure am. When I can find the time, that is. The Road Knights are down to meeting once a month now that we are all working stiffs. Have you decided to join us?"

"No," John caught himself, "not exactly. Actually, I'm planning to join the MARC racing circuit this spring."

"Oh, yeah, I read about that new racing association," Mark answered. "Good for you. That will give you great exposure, not to mention experience."

"I'm looking for a pit crew," John cut him short.

Mark glanced over at the cashier, unoccupied at the moment and giving her rapt attention to their conversation."

Mark quieted his voice. "Come back to the office for a moment."

John followed through the large double doors leading into the unheated storeroom and loading dock, past the time clock, and into a small office cluttered with stacks of paper.

Mark sat behind the desk and spoke first. "I know; you're looking for a few good mechanics to keep your coupe in top form."

"Not the coupe. It's a new car circuit. I need someone to pit me during the races when I'm on the road. Pop has to manage his shop and can't travel to the races. Besides, I need a younger guy to back me up."

"Want me to ask the guys if anyone is interested?"

"I'm asking you. If anyone else is available, we can talk."

Mark shook his head. "I don't know. Traveling around the Midwest all summer isn't exactly a bright career move. Who's going to stock the lettuce and make sure there's enough Velveeta on the shelves if I'm in small town America spilling gas into your tank? Can you really expect me to leave all this behind?" Mark stretched his arms and almost touched the adjacent walls in his cramped office.

John laughed, then he realized Mark was only half joking.

"Tell you what," Mark began, "I've watched you and I believe you're going places, but I'm still figuring out what I want to be when I grow up. How about if I sleep on it and get back with you?"

"That's all I can ask," John replied. "Don't think too long. I'm looking for a right-hand man who's ready to pursue NASCAR with me. It's going to be an interesting ride."

Mark nodded and shook John's hand. "I appreciate it. Speaking of hands, yours are like ice. We have a few pair of gloves in the housewares aisle."

John purchased a pair of black gloves on the way out and quickly strode back toward Pop's Garage. Mark would do it. John could see how Mark's eyes sparked at the mention of NASCAR, despite his attempt to hide any reaction. He was probably celebrating in his office right now, shouting and throwing those stacks of paper around the room.

John circled the black Hudson Hornet for the third time. He had considered the short-bodied '53 Dodge with its L-head engine, yet it lacked the power he craved. The Lincoln was tempting, but it was too plush and considerably out of his price range, as was the Super 88 Rocket Olds. He made a good salary at the mill and was able to tuck almost half of each paycheck in a savings account without Helen's knowledge. Then there was the money he had stashed away working for Pop throughout high school. Those few dollars

D. T. Dignan

a week added up, but John was frugal and wanted the most power his money could buy without all the glamour and frills. Buicks were too ostentatious, and while the Chevy sport coupe fell neatly in his budget, it lacked guts under the hood. No, the Hudson was ahead by a long shot. If it was good enough for NASCAR Cup Series champions Herb Thomas in '51 and Tim Flock in '52, then it was a smart choice for John Powers in '53.

The Hornet's lower center of gravity and flowing, aerodynamic body style made it ideal for racing. A combination of the 308-cubic-inch, six-cylinder L-head engine and twin H power carburetors helped the engine "breathe" better than its larger V-8 counterparts. This baby could crank out 160 horsepower and top 107 miles an hour. The two-piece windshield was old school, but he could live with that. The center-mount radio antenna would have to go. Unfortunately, the $2,200-price tag was more than he could pay. There was the lower-priced Jet, but it sported only a 202-cubic-inch engine under the hood. No, he had to have the Hornet.

"I'll give you $1,700 cash for the Hornet," John offered the dealer.

"Are you kidding? The Jet starts at $1,890!"

John paused in contemplation before responding. He had a little more than the $1,700 but knew enough to start lower. After that offer, anything would sound good.

"Think of it this way. I'm offering you cash for this car. Not credit, cash. No worries about my qualifying for a loan or making payments on time. You don't have to spend time and energy chasing me down when I'm a month late on the payments. Everyone else comes in here looking for installments. I think a cash sale is worth at least fifteen percent, don't you?" He had him there. The salesman was crunching numbers in his head.

"That's still lower than the Jet. I can't go that low."

"You know, we get a number of customers at Pop's Garage who decide it's time for a new car. It would be nice to have a relationship with a trustworthy dealership to send them to."

"I, I don't know."

John persisted. "I'm standing here ready to buy this car for cash, and you're comparing the price to a car I don't want. Guess I'll have to revisit the Dodge dealer. He offered to throw in overdrive."

John turned to leave. Not inclined to lose the sale, the dealer spoke up. "How about $1,980 cash sale? That's ten percent off the original price."

John pondered. It was more than the $1,800 cash he had brought with him. However, if he raided the rent money in the bureau drawer, there would be enough. The Hudson gleamed under the white lights of the car lot and for a moment John relived the rush of finding his old rusted coupe, a vestige of possibility and hope, now stored at the garage for posterity. There was no walking away.

"I'll give you $1,980 cash for the car if you throw in a little paint job from the body shop."

The dealer glanced at the Hudson. "You don't like black?"

"I just need a few personalized touches."

"Done."

Two days later and cash poor, John eased the Hudson out of the lot. Though shining black and stunning, she seemed nondescript compared with the more elegant Buicks, Olds, Fords, and Chevrolets that lined the dealers' lots on the way home, save for the large white "23" on each door and the words "John "Powerhouse" Powers" inscribed over the side windows.

Chapter Eleven

READY TO GET ON the road for his Midwest adventure, John tossed a modest suitcase into the Hudson and slammed the trunk shut. His one-man pit crew, Mark, waited silently near the passenger door for John to finish his good-byes. Mrs. Grant stood on the sidewalk with her very pregnant daughter. John was glad Helen's mother was there; It made him feel less guilt about leaving for the MARC tour. Dr. Grant was not present. He avoided John at all cost. The last words John remembered his new father-in-law sharing were at the wedding reception. "Just keep your pants zipped and everything will be fine" was the gist of it. Helen struggled to be pleasant and upbeat, offering a false smile on this sunny May afternoon full of spring birdsong and cool crisp breezes. John could hear the strain in her voice and see the fear in her eyes. She didn't want him to leave. To John, the reason for her anxiety was less about having the baby alone than it was about his racing. She had been trying to talk him out of going for weeks, bringing up every mishap in the history of the sport as examples.

He gave her a gentle squeeze and softly kissed her lips. "It won't be long, and I'll send my winnings."

"It's not that, Johnny. I just hope the baby comes when you're close by so you can be here." There were races in Ohio and Pennsylvania that would require only a few hours' drive for John to stop home. Whether he would be at those tracks to coincide with the timing of the birth was questionable.

Mrs. Grant chimed in, "You know your father and I are here for you. It will be all right. I'm sure John will check in with us every day."

John knew this was meant as a command rather than a suggestion. "That's right." John stepped toward the car. "I'll call you. You know where the money is, in the top bureau drawer?" Helen nodded. He said it more to appease her mother than to remind Helen; he wanted Mrs. Grant to know he wasn't leaving his wife destitute. Of course, he didn't expound on how much was left.

John and Mark hopped in the Hudson and headed down the road, John waving from his open window.

"Be careful!" Helen called out as they pulled away. "Remember Langhorne."

"You bastard," Mark joked to John, "leaving your wife when she's about to pop any day."

"She's not due for another three weeks. She'll be fine. Her father's a doctor, for God's sake."

"Hmm. You make a good point there. Why should they need you?"

"Exactly."

"I mean, after all, you're just the kid's father."

"Do you want to do this or not?"

Mark laughed. "Do you think I'd be sitting here with my duds in your trunk if I didn't want to be here? Do you think I would have given up my promising career at the A&P if I didn't want to be here?"

"Okay, okay. I just don't need you to get on my back about Helen."

"It's a deal. I won't mention a word. At least for another ten miles. By the way, what did she mean by 'remember Langhorne'?"

"There was a bad crack-up at Langhorne Speedway in '51. Modified stocks, the famous sixty-second wreck. There were collisions, rollovers, fire, car parts flying everywhere, you name it."

"So, she's worried you're going to crash."

"Yeah. I don't know why she has to focus on the negative. You know why that crash is famous? With all the torn-up metal and smoke, the only injury was a broken leg. She's trying to subtly undermine my career by planting fear and worry. Women are good at that, you know. Why else would she want to put bad thoughts into my head before a race?"

"I doubt she thinks of it that way. She's just worried because she loves you and doesn't want to see you get hurt. Why, I don't know."

John never could tell if Mark was joking or making a jab at him, but he was all John had for support during the circuit and would have to put up with his wry sense of humor. None of the other Road Knights were able to get away. As needed, John would scare up other crewmembers from the local race mechanics and race enthusiasts at each track.

May 10, 1953, turned out to be a beautiful day in Ohio. The Dayton Speedway hosted twenty-four cars and almost ten thousand spectators for the inaugural MARC new car division race. Arriving the day before, John was pleased to find how well the Hudson handled on the half-mile, paved track. He had never raced on pavement and didn't miss the ruts and dust, though he wouldn't be able to use his power slide technique on the turns. The Hudson was smooth and powerful but much larger than the coupe. It took every ounce of concentration he had to squeeze past the cars ahead, and he found the cars behind riding his draft more readily.

Perhaps it was a combination of mastering a new car and the first time on a paved and banked oval that caused John to come in twelfth place.

"What's the matter," Mark scoffed after the race, "afraid to scratch the paint on your new car?"

With the strain of starting the MARC tour with stiffer competition, a new car, no money, and many strange tracks ahead on the sixteen-race circuit, John's nerves were on edge and the comment wasn't taken well.

John grabbed Mark's shirt in his clenched fist and pulled him inches within his angered face. "Don't you start with me! You couldn't handle racing if you tried … Who are you to comment on my driving?"

Mark backed down and lifted his arms apologetically. "Okay, okay, I'm just toying with you. Geez, are we a little high strung or what?"

"Just remember, you're here to support me," John snapped as he released his grip. "If I wanted negative talk, I would have stayed home." It took a few moments for John to cool down and he shook the anger off his shoulders.

"Speaking of which," Mark interjected, "you'd better call Helen when we get back to the room. It's been two days since you phoned."

"That's why I love you; not only can you pit but you're a good mom too."

Frankly, John didn't want to call Helen until after the Canfield race. Canfield was closer to home. He didn't want to risk her talking him into coming home before the race was run. He felt confident about Canfield, a track he had run many Saturdays while earning qualification for the MARC new car tour. This was one race he felt provided an advantage, and he wanted to run it with no distractions.

The Dayton race over, drivers packed up their gear and their teams—those who could afford it lifted their racers onto trailers pulled by other cars or trucks—and independently they moved on to Canfield, Ohio's quarter-mile dirt track, for the next race.

The idea of taking a detour and stopping home before reaching their destination plagued John as he drove on, Mark lost in his own thoughts in the passenger seat. Why was this eating him up? Helen knew what to expect—that he may not be back right away. While there was time to visit for a day or two, he feared Helen would lay on the guilt and he would feel obligated to give up the circuit and stay home. Worse, she would fill his head with negative thoughts about crashes and near misses. No, it was best if he stayed away. He needed to set a precedent. This was his career, and it had to come first. His absence for a few months during the spring and summer was not the end of the world. If he caved now, his driving future would be over and he'd be back to eating red-hot sparks at the steel mill.

Canfield was kinder to the kid from Pittsburgh in his black Hudson. He made fourth place and earned modest winnings for his efforts. He was relieved to have something to send to Helen, though he would need to hold back enough for a new set of tires and meals, and to pay a few local guys to help pit at the next race. Fortunately, Mark had agreed to half of his pay upfront, which John had provided prior to leaving Pittsburgh, and the other half at the conclusion of the tour in return for meals and lodging, when they could afford it.

Aside from the money, the Canfield race had returned his confidence and aggressive driving stance.

Warm, yellow sunlight spilled into the Hudson and roused John awake. His neck was stiff and sore from lying in the same position all night—knees bent to allow his long frame room to lie across the front seat. Mark's soft breathing rose and fell from the backseat as John's eyes focused. He stared at the roof's interior for a few moments and then followed down to the window, cracked open just enough to let some air in, bright with daylight. Once his eyes adjusted, he saw a little, black face peering at him through the glass. Startled, he sat up quickly and peered back. The face retreated a few feet.

"Who's there?" John asked groggily, rubbing his neck. "What do you want?"

"I, I didn't mean to scare you, mister," came a child's voice.

Mark groaned in the backseat and sat up.

A much larger figure in a flower-print approached the car behind the boy. "Jack, what are you doing staring at those men? Let them be."

"It's a racecar, Momma!" the child squealed.

"Well, it's parked right now and in front of my house." Momma bent over to peer into the car. "Please excuse my son, he's only three and doesn't know better. Got to admit, you do have a strange-looking car."

John smiled shyly, opened the door, exited, and stretched.

"I apologize if we are intruding," John began, "but this looked like a nice, quiet spot to stop for the night. We're on our way to the next race in Flat Rock. We'll be leaving now."

"Now just a moment," Momma protested, "you mean you and your friend slept here last night—in the car?"

Mark crawled from the backseat, wrinkled shirt and tousled hair suggesting a night of tossing and turning.

"We're a bit short on funds to pay for both a room and food, so we chose eating over comfort," Mark replied.

"Where are you all from?" Momma asked.

"Pittsburgh."

"Well, now. This is Michigan and we can't have visitors sleeping in the streets. Poppa and I have an extra room. You'll stay with us."

"Oh, we couldn't impose—" John was quickly cut off.

"I won't hear of it. No sleepin' in the car in front of this house when there's a perfectly good bed to be had. If you

143

want to pay for the room, you can run up to the market and fetch me some milk and groceries."

Mark and John glanced at each other. John shrugged. Why not? It would be more comfortable and they had nowhere else to be until tomorrow's race.

"It's a deal."

Jack stood partially hidden behind his mother, arms wrapped around her leg.

"Good. Well then, if you are to stay with us, we must be formally introduced. I'm Oneida Miller."

"John Powers. And this is my friend, Mark Underwood. Where's your grocery list?"

"Come on inside and I'll write it down."

They headed for the house, doorway full of one old man and three children watching with interest. "We're having company stay the night, Poppa."

Poppa, apparently Oneida's father, chuckled and shook his head.

"I don't know how we can thank you for your hospitality," Mark exclaimed between mouthfuls of sweet hotcake. "First that wonderful chicken dinner, putting us up for the night, and now this sumptuous breakfast."

John thought Mark was laying it on a bit thick, but nodded in agreement. "We appreciate everything you've done."

Oneida Miller gave a wry smile and winked at her youngest son who was literally bouncing in his seat. The other children glanced at each other and giggled. It was evident a conspiracy was under way.

"Well, since you like my home cookin' so much, there is a way you can pay me back."

"What's that?" John wondered.

"Take my babies for a ride in that racing machine of yours," she answered. "Ah, a nice, *slow* ride that is."

Little Jack looked like he would combust with excitement.

"Sure, I can do that. We'll take a spin right after breakfast."

Jack let out a laugh that qualified as the most joyous sound John had ever heard.

John and Mark headed out front followed by four children. Within moments, the entire block seemed to have gathered to see number 23 in action.

"Whose gonna ride in the front seat?"

"I say it's me. Ladies first."

"You always get your way! I say it's me 'cause I'm the oldest!"

"No. Me! I'm the littlest!"

Their mother, tired of the ruckus, piped in. "Why don't you settle it by drawing straws?"

The oldest child ran to the neighbor's backyard to raid the hen house and returned clutching a fistful of straws. He held them out to his compatriots; each in turn pulled a straw and held it up, quickly comparing to the others. The lone girl in the group flashed a bright smile at pulling the seemingly shortest straw.

"It's my turn! I wanna pick one!" whined the smallest.

"Okay, keep your shirt on, Jack," said his older brother as he lowered his hand.

The littlest fan quickly plucked a straw from this brother's hand and his brown eyes grew in excitement. "I win! I win!" he squealed and jumped, dropping the two-inch straw on the pavement while the other children moaned.

"Pile in," John instructed as he opened the passenger door. He had never seen kids move so fast. His backseat was crowded to capacity, eager faces peering from every window. He smiled as he thought what their faces would look like whizzing around the track at top speed.

The smallest boy climbed in the front seat, his thin legs poking straight out toward the dash.

"You can go now, Mr. Racer," he was anxious. John slid behind the wheel and grabbed the helmet being handed to him by the backseat crew.

"I have to put my helmet on first. Every racer wears a helmet."

"Okay," the little voice replied. Eight pairs of eyes watched intently as John turned the key. This was so much simpler than his coupe, which required easing out the choke and pressing a starter button. The Hudson sputtered and shook as the engine strained to start but refused to roar to life.

"Must have flooded the engine," John reasoned. He waited a few moments and tried again. The little face in the front seat stared up hopefully at John, praying. Again, the Hudson puttered and choked. The children's grandfather shuffled over and peered in at John, rapping on the glass with the handle of his cane until John lowered the window.

"Hey Mr. *Puh puh puh pa puh* Powers. Having engine trouble?" The old man's clever way of mimicking the sound of John's car brought a burst of laughter from the backseat.

Grandpa *he-he'd* at his own joke. John just shook his head until he saw Mark approaching with a large, red gas can.

"Sorry, buddy, I left her dry after yesterday's milk run." Mark quickly poured the fuel into the tank. His job done, he walked past John and mumbled in his ear, "Keep it a short ride, we only have enough cash for one more fill-up to get us through the next race."

John nodded and tried the engine a third time. She roared and settled into a soft rumble to the passengers' lively cheers and onlookers' applause.

"Hurray!" the little voice cried from the front seat as the coupe rumbled down the street and disappeared from view.

Two hours and many good-byes later, John and Mark drove toward the track. John laughed and rattled the coins in his pocket.

"We have gas money, now."

"I have to admit that was pretty shrewd, charging all those little kids a quarter for a ride in the Hudson. How can you live with yourself?"

"Thirty-five cents for the front seat," John corrected. "They loved it. I could have charged a dollar and they would have broken their piggy banks. We even had a few adults join in. They will tell their kids that they rode in the famous John Power's number 23."

Mark snickered. "It's so refreshing, being around someone with such a humble, modest view of himself."

"It's true. Just wait."

"Yeah, you'd better do something with this race or we'll be sleeping in the car again."

"I'm gaining experience toward NASCAR. You don't have to remind me what we're here for."

"Say, you forgot to call Helen yesterday. Better find a phone before the race."

A steady rain pelted the phone booth glass as the rotary dial clicked John's home number. The Hudson waited outside the Howard Johnson's where Mark sat finishing his pie and coffee. It was six rings before the call was answered, but Helen's voice was not on the other end.

"John, it's Beverly." Upon hearing his voice, Helen's mother sounded restless.

"Yes, hi, can you get Helen for me, please?"

"Helen's not here, John. She had the baby and is still at the hospital."

John's stomach turned. "When?"

"Two days ago. She began labor around two o'clock in the afternoon and her father drove her to the hospital. The baby came around six hours later. We didn't know how to reach you, John, so I've been staying at the house waiting for your call."

John didn't know how to respond. "Is … is …"

"Helen is just fine. You have a beautiful son. His name is Michael. That is what you and Helen discussed for a boy, Michael?" Her voice had softened. John knew that Beverly wanted to accept him, to make up for the bitterness of Helen's father and to morally support her only daughter.

"Yes, Michael." John twisted the phone cord round and round the fingers of his free hand to stop the shaking.

Beverly's voice came through the phone receiver, but John struggled to focus on her words.

"He's a healthy boy, weighed eight pounds, seven ounces, and has a head of dark hair just like yours. And you should see his eyes! As dark blue as midnight."

"That's great. Just great," John stammered.

"Helen will be staying at our place for a while so I can help her adjust to caring for the baby and so she will not be alone. You'll have to call her there. John, John, do you know when you might be able to get home?"

This was a difficult question. They were currently en route from Michigan to Indiana and would be at the farthest point from home.

"It's hard to say. I'm calling from the road on the way to Indiana. I'll check the race schedule and see what I can work out."

"Good. Let us know as soon as you can. I'll send Helen your love. She misses you something terrible, John."

"Yes. Tell Helen I love her and will call again tomorrow."

The receiver clicked in place and John stood silent for a moment, only the sound of rain pattering against the glass. He untangled his hand from the twisted black cord and tried to picture a small baby with deep blue eyes and dark hair cradled in Helen's arms. The thought grabbed him by the throat until he could not stifle the sobs that racked his chest. John's hands covered his face as he slid against the phone booth wall toward the floor and crumpled in the corner.

"Oh, God. Oh, God." His very soul was full of the wonder of it—of a human person that had entered the world because of him and Helen, a person totally dependent on him from a woman who loved him enough to give up her own dreams to make it happen. He was missing it. Helen had gone through labor when he was avoiding calling her so as not to disrupt his plans.

At that moment, his feelings for Helen were more than he could withstand. He sat there for several minutes until the tears stopped and he could compose himself. John dried his red eyes on his plaid shirtsleeve and was thankful for the rain that would hide his tear-stained face. He didn't need Mark to see him like this.

He slowly approached the restaurant and pulled out his wallet to pay the bill. "Hey, good news." His voice was upbeat. "I'm a father."

Mark stood from his seat at the counter and slapped John on the back, a wide grin plastering his face.

"It's a boy … Michael," John added.

Overhearing the news, the restaurant patrons broke into applause and whistles.

John paid the bill and waved as he and Mark went out the door. "Sorry I have no cigars."

A message waited for John at the motel desk. It was from Momma and it wasn't good news. Helen and the baby had been evicted from their home and would need to stay with her parents until further notice. There was not enough money in the bureau to pay the rent, now two months overdue with the third month due in a few days. Could he send money?

Mark was incredulous. "You didn't pay the rent before you left?"

"I needed all the cash I could get my hands on to buy the Hudson. Don't you get it? This is an investment. This car *is* my income. We've done all right. Our winnings will be enough to cover rent for six months, and that's after I pay your salary. I can't believe the landlord would kick us out after missing only two payments. As soon as we're back in Pennsylvania, I'll give everything I've got to Helen for the bills. I just need more time."

"That's another week away," Mark reminded. Do you think your parents would help in the meantime?"

John shook his head. "No, I wouldn't ask them. Momma has only pin money, and Dad's still pissed that I quit the mill to join the MARC circuit. He hasn't spoken to me since April."

"What about Pop?"

That was tempting … He knew Pop would help John with anything. It just didn't smell right, going to Pop to bail him out again. No. He wanted to prove to everyone that he was an adult and could handle his own problems. He told Mark as much.

"Give me the key," Mark snapped.

"The room key?"

"No, the key to the Hudson. I need to get out for a while. Go … somewhere."

John sneered. "Do you think I'm going to let you take off with the car? Forget it?"

"Either I take this car, without you in it, or you can find someone else to order around for the rest of the circuit. I'm done."

"Done? What do you mean 'done'? You made an agreement. Besides, how're you going to get home with no car?

"There are ways. Taxi, bus, train, you name it. Maybe Helen would come pick me up."

John shook his head and fingered the key in his pocket. What was wrong with Mark? He never blew up like this.

"Just tell me where you're going with my car and I'll consider it."

"I don't know where I'm going, I just need to get out for a while, get away—away from you."

John threw the fob at Mark so that it smacked him in the chest. "Here, take a joy ride. Just know this: anything happens to that car and you're dead."

Seven hours later and Mark had not returned. John lay on the bed in his motel room, watching the black-and-white television screen flickering in the growing evening dimness, getting angrier with each passing minute. He had not eaten since they arrived—had no car to travel the five miles to the nearest restaurant and didn't feel like walking. He wanted to be there when Mark returned, *if* he returned. Mark wasn't the type to pull a stunt like driving home with the car, but he was pretty hot. John took assurance in what he knew about Mark's general disposition and loyalty. The odds were high that he would pull up to the motel before too long. In the meantime, he was out there burning up precious gas and subjecting the Hudson to who knew what. Mark didn't drink, so the thought of him stopping at a bar, getting toasted, and driving only crossed John's mind momentarily before he dismissed it.

The bed stand phone shrilled, causing John to jump at the sudden noise. "John, I'm so glad you came through. I knew it was just a misunderstanding." Helen's voice was breathless.

"What?"

"The wire! Thank you for sending the money to pay the rent—we just left the Western Union office. I've been staying with my parents since Michael was born but wanted to go to the house before you returned so we could all be together as a family on your first day back. The eviction notice said we had to have all our furniture out by the end of the month. Johnny, I was so scared. I just phoned the landlady in Florida and explained. She didn't know we had the baby, John, and was so apologetic. She really is a nice person. I'm sending her a check tomorrow and we will be paid through June."

Mark. John closed his eyes and rubbed his aching forehead.

"You're acting so fast. Well, it meant a lot to me because it helped Daddy to be less angry."

"That's great, Helen."

"John, I'm so anxious for you to come home next week and to see Michael. He really does look like you."

"Yes, I'm excited too. Helen, I've had some success with the circuit and have won a decent pot of money." The part about the money wasn't entirely true, but he needed to make his pursuit sound good. "This is the year to qualify for NASCAR. I can feel it."

"I'm glad for you, John." Helen's voice had quieted. "Please, just come home to me as soon as you can."

The conversation had ended. John clicked off the television and sat in the darkness. Yes, he had Mark pegged pretty well. Within an hour, a small knock came to the door and John answered to see Mark dangling the Hudson keys in front of him.

"Have you been out at all?" Mark asked.

"Nope. Just been sitting here watching *Dragnet*, waiting for you." He took the key and dropped it in his trousers pocket.

"There's a pretty decent diner a few miles up the road, having a special on pot roast. I've eaten, but you may want to check it out."

John nodded. "I'll do that."

Mark turned to head for his own room.

"Mark," John said. "I talked to Helen."

"She called you?" Mark seemed nervous.

"Yeah, called to thank me for the money. Why'd you do it?"

Marked shrugged. "It was just the right thing to do."

John pulled out his wallet and flipped through several bills that he handed to Mark.

"Doesn't leave you with much," Mark said.

"Don't worry. I plan to pick up more where that came from."

Chapter Twelve

JOHN WIPED HIS SOILED hands on a rag and rolled from underneath the Dodge he was greasing. Cool April mist swirled in the thick air outside Pop's Garage. It had been a steady morning with every bay full and a few more jobs waiting in the lot. Now the shop was closed and the garage was fairly quiet as John, Pop, and Smitty were all engrossed in separate projects. Pop kept crawling under a Chevy diagnosed with power-glide transmission problems. The Pennsylvania hills could wreak havoc on transmissions.

Libbey padded between the three mechanics, staring at her chosen subject until they provided a soft word or a pat on the head. Momentarily satisfied, she would take her large body to her bed and stretch out, yawn, and dose for a while.

John was lost in his thoughts about the upcoming racing season. NASCAR was hosting four Grand National races in Pennsylvania in 1954, one only about twenty-five miles north in Sharon, which he planned to be a part of. Just the thought of being on the same track with Lee Petty, Herb Thomas, and Buck Baker gave him heart palpitations. He'd have to be careful. Crossing circuits to earn points was frowned upon, and he could have his MARC points stripped away if he got caught. Yet the intrigue of running a NASCAR race, and the fact that he had the skill and experience to do it, made his mind up. He would register for the NASCAR race under a pseudonym—paint the new name on the car. This could work. He tossed names around in his mind to see how they fit. None had the ring to them that Powerhouse held.

John had barely made it to his feet when a loud bang behind him made him jump and spin around. He was horrified to see the Chevy had fallen.

"Help," a weak voice cried out from under the car. The lower half of Pop's body protruded from under the car, just behind the front tire.

John and Smitty scuttled to raise the heavy, steel front end, trying to lift with their own strength and coming up short. "Hold on Pop, hold on," John said as he grabbed a spare jack and positioned it under the front end of the Chevy and pumped with all his might. The car slowly lifted and Smitty shoved two jack stands under the frame to hold it in place. Pop gasped from underneath.

"Help me get him out." Smitty was pulling on Pop's ankles but, being a small man, was unable to pull Pop to freedom, who had not used a creeper. Libbey, startled by the commotion, now paced along the side of the car. John grabbed one leg and Smitty the other, pulling until Pop was out from underneath the Chevy. He groaned and rolled to his side, gasping for breath, his face pale and moist.

"Call an ambulance!" John hollered, and Smitty, wide-eyed, ran to the front desk.

John dropped to the cold, cement floor next to his friend and wrapped his arms around the older man's shoulders, lifting him gently onto his lap. Pop wheezed and groaned in pain. John pulled the soiled cap from Pop's head and tossed it aside, and then he loosened the top two shirt buttons around Pop's neck, waiting and watching until Pop's breathing became less labored. Libbey stood next to the pair, licking and nuzzling Pop's face until John had to push her away.

"That's a nice girl, my girl," Pop wheezed.

Smitty returned. "They're on the way." Then looking down at Pop, he said, "You're going to be all right."

"Yes." Pop nodded. "Better now. Couldn't breathe. Fell on my chest, my face."

John found himself stroking Pop's head as it lay in his lap. Without a thought, he bent down and kissed the top of Pop's head, which was now returning to a normal shade of pink through his thinning hair. John leaned over and peered under the Chevy to survey where Pop had lain and how the car could have fallen. Pop had done the right thing. There was the jack stand, though only one, perched under the car, two of its legs snapped where rust had set it. Its top was crumpled and bent. Good thing Pop had not used a creeper; it would have served only to leave less space between the Chevy and the ground. Old. Old, rusty, faulty equipment. If he had the money, there would be hydraulic lifts in each bay, and there would be no more crawling under cars. He would do it, as soon as he made enough from NASCAR. He would totally refit Pop's Garage with the latest of everything. He owed the old man at least that much.

A siren wailed softly in the distance, traveling on the thick, wet air, growing louder and louder until an ambulance stopped at the door.

What was it about that smell, that hospital smell, that turned John's stomach? Whatever it was, John hated it. The last time he set foot in a hospital was when Susan died. Just seeing the place caused the same sick feeling to emerge from the pit of his gut.

A uniformed nurse looked up from her station as John approached, holding a bag with a half dozen bakery muffins tucked under his arm.

"I'm looking for Pop," he stated. The nurse gave him a confused look.

"What's the name?"

John was embarrassed. "Pop … of Pop's Garage." The nurse stared back, unresponsive. "The guy who had the car fall on him," John responded impatiently.

A glimmer of recognition, then she said, "Follow me."

John followed the white cap and dress down a long corridor to the very last room on the right. Pop lay in bed, propped slightly upright and gazing out the window.

"Powerhouse!" He was in full voice now.

John flopped in the one available chair. "I brought you some muffins. Figured you'd be hungry since you missed lunch."

"Ah." Pop chuckled and pulled a morsel from the white paper bag. "Thank you. I am. Were you able to close up?"

"Yep, everything's pinned down. Libbey's fed and has the place under control. Smitty and I will stop in tomorrow for a few hours after church. We'll be caught up by Monday."

Pop polished off his muffin and offered the bag to John, who shook his head.

"I don't know what I would have done without you both. If I had been there alone …"

John quickly changed the subject. "I phoned Momma. I told her you would be all right or she would have been there before the ambulance. She and Dad will be by in a few hours to check on you." Pop folded the top of his muffin bag shut and placed it on the bed stand. "So what did the doctor say?" John continued. "*Is* everything all right?"

"Well, nothing's broken. Just contusions—and pain. I'm going to be black and blue for a while. There was just enough room under that car to flatten the air out of me. It happened so fast. Thank God, I stayed clear of the wheels. I don't understand how that car fell; I had it secured."

A worried look crossed Pop's face, a look of self-doubt.

"The jack stand failed, just crumpled," said John. "It had rusted. We need to get you better equipment."

Pop looked away as if deep in thought. "The equipment *is* getting older. So am I."

"When can you go home?"

"Tomorrow afternoon. Have to make sure there's no internal bleeding or clotting; they want to watch things for a while. Guess I'm on twenty-four-hour surveillance."

A nurse entered the room. "Do I smell cake? Are you having a party in here?" she mused. "Time to take your vitals, Mr. Vogt."

Vogt? John was intrigued. He had never heard Pop referred to as anything other than Pop. What was his first name? He stood behind the nurse and peered over her shoulder at the chart. "Vogt, Max" was written across the top.

John felt very much in the way and wanted to leave as the nurse started fussing around Pop, wrapping a blood-pressure cuff on his arm. "I'm going to head out. I'll come by tomorrow and pick you up, Max."

Pop snapped to attention at hearing his true name. His eyes, deep and touched with a bit of sadness, searched John's face for a moment, then he smiled.

"I'll be ready."

John couldn't leave the hospital fast enough. He practically ran through the parking lot to his Hudson, sighing as the car rolled through the parking lot and toward home.

He felt anger, the chronic, frustrating anger that makes you want to punch your fist through a wall, tinged with a deep sadness. He wasn't sure why. Pop would be fine. It could have been much worse. Perhaps it was that Pop was alone. Sure, he had the guys at the shop and was friends with John's folks, but he had no one at home. No, it was different. Somehow, hearing Pop's name had triggered a new thought, a realization that this man John had known since early childhood actually had a persona outside his relationship with John and his family. John sensed that, during his entire life, his relationship with Pop was really all about himself … how Pop related to him, what Pop could do for him. The man named Max Vogt had devoted himself entirely to John and had invested his time, his money, and his knowledge, more so than anyone else. Rather than spending his cash on updated equipment for his shop, he was spending it on restoring the coupe or in giving John raises so he could afford to race. Max Vogt had been influencing and grooming his Powerhouse for years. And John didn't even know his name.

Should it matter?

The look on Pop's face when John called him Max confirmed that it did.

John walked briskly down the hallway toward Pop's room, more upbeat now. After leaving church with Helen and Michael, he and Smitty put in several hours at the shop and were able to breeze through the remaining projects. He had phoned his parents the night before with an idea that had him so excited that he felt he would burst until it was put in action. The whole town knew Pop; why not take up a collection to help fund a hydraulic lift for at least one of the bays for undercarriage work? Momma would take up a collection with the help of her woman's group at church and Dad had many contacts at the mill. John planned a secret strategy that involved spying on competing garages to see what they were charging. Pop's "best prices" in town perhaps needed some inflation to better equip the shop. As long as they were still within the competition, the customers would continue to support a well-run and friendly shop that had been in town for decades.

Too bad he couldn't reach Maggie. She could weasel information out of some poor, unsuspecting mechanic better than anyone else he knew. It would all be a surprise. He would try to get Pop out of the shop so the lift could be installed; maybe a road trip to a race would do it.

Even the hospital looked better, the setting evening sun splashing through the windows of each room he passed. He landed at Pop's doorway and walked in—to an empty room. The bed had been stripped and cleaned. For a moment John felt disoriented; it was too much like what had happened to Susan. No, he took a deep breath and reasoned that perhaps someone else had come earlier and taken him home already. Maybe he was in the bathroom.

John walked to the nurses' station. "I'm here to pick up Max Vogt."

The nurse stood and came around the counter.

John felt his heart begin to race and his face flush.

"Mr. Vogt is doing fine right now. He has been moved to another floor and …"

"Moved? But he's supposed to go home today."

The nurse caught the eye of a doctor as he walked toward the station and motioned for him to join the conversation. "This young man is here to pick up Mr. Vogt."

The doctor nodded and offered his hand. Then he began to explain.

"Mr. Vogt is going to be staying with us for a little while longer. He had a mild ischemic stroke last night; a blood clot from his chest injury entered the brain and has resulted in numbness in his legs and weakness of his left side. He has been put on blood thinners, and we are monitoring him closely."

Seeing John's eyes widen at the mention of a stroke, he continued. "Would you like to see him?"

John padded behind the doctor down a long corridor and up the elevator to a room with considerably more medical paraphernalia than the previous room.

An IV bag hung next to the bed with tubes leading to Pop's arm. Pop appeared as John had never seen him before: ghostly pale, weak, and tired. He seemed smaller than John remembered. His lids lifted slowly as he gazed at John, offered a little smile, and then with a quiet, raspy voice said, "Hey, Powerhouse. I'm going to be late for our date."

Chapter Thirteen

HELEN WAS HAPPIER THAN she had been in a long time. John arrived home from the garage at eight o'clock each weeknight to Helen's bright attitude and dinner ready. Some days, he wondered if she forced her mood to be pleasant and accommodating so that he would stay close to home. No one could fake it every day; her sunny disposition must be original. The scent of pot roast or baked chicken greeted him at the door just moments before his wife, usually wearing a brightly colored dress and heels and with her face and hair done up, appeared. She was pregnant again—two months—and John knew she felt more secure with him holding a steady job as chief mechanic and part owner of Pop's Garage. The steel mill wouldn't hire him back after he abandoned them for the MARC circuit. John had slid into the role at the garage since Pop's accident.

John also knew Helen loved watching him interact with Michael, something he had not done since his son's birth. John had to admit he enjoyed having his little man curl up on his lap for an after-dinner story or radio program or watching Michael try to race his plastic cars down the hallway. Though barely a toddler, the boy clearly thought his father walked on water, and it was nice having a personal admiration society.

It was June, and John was sticking to racing on the weekends and closer to home. He had to. Racing in the MARC circuit this summer was out of the question. Pop was getting around, but barely. His left side remained weak and unpredictable from the stroke, and he needed a cane to walk. Though Pop never complained of pain, John noticed he tossed aspirin down his throat several times a day. Crawling under cars and stretching into engine cavities was doable, but laborious and tiring.

The secret fundraiser had brought in over three hundred dollars, which was not quite enough to install the hydraulic lift. Even driving the tow truck was problematic. The strain of offering "the best service in town" was beginning to wear on Pop. Even the most loyal customers became aggravated if their ride wasn't ready as soon as possible. Pop needed the younger men to do most of the shop work while he handled the finances, purchasing of parts, and pouring coffee for those who wished to wait while the quicker services were completed. The only one who benefited from the situation was Libbey. Pop had more time to toss her ball in the yard adjacent to the garage or stroke her soft, black head as she sat behind the counter watching him write up a service ticket.

Yes, both girls were happier. John was tired and felt he had settled to keep the peace. NASCAR seemed even further out of reach. If not for the weekend races and his local successes, he would have been miserable.

The only person who was truly miserable these days was Murphy. John's absence due to the MARC new car circuit the previous summer had left Murphy as the chief contender at the Pennsylvania and Ohio tracks. Now John Powers was faster and more skilled, and with his Hudson Hornet, he was placing ahead of Murphy's Ford in every race. Other than an occasional jab at an after-race party at the local pub, the two men never spoke. Murphy liked to talk hard and drink harder. John's idea of a good time was more about having a few laughs and going home after two beers. He saved his attitude for the track. Murphy knew John hated him; that was sufficient.

John splashed cool water on his eyes before the drive home. He had worked into the night tuning and prepping the Hudson for the next day's race at Heidelberg. Business at the garage was booming. That was a good problem to have, but it left John precious little time to keep his racecar in top form. Customer work kept him going until past ten before he could turn his attention to the Hudson. He couldn't expect Smitty to put in the kind of hours John was keeping. The last thing John needed was to burn out his best mechanic. While he could hire a novice mechanic to handle the routine work like oil changes and replacing tires, it would mean less income for him. He needed all he could get his hands on to feed his hungry racing appetite.

Satisfied that the Hudson was ready for the occasion, John prepared to lock up the garage and head home. It was after 1:00 a.m. and he hoped Helen had saved some leftovers. The bathroom light at the back of the shop was kept burning as a night light for Libbey, who was curled on her sizeable bed in the corner of the garage. John pulled his keys from his trousers pocket and headed toward the door to his waiting Buick, but Libbey rose and gave a soft whine. She stared intently at the door leading to the waiting area and let out a low, soft growl.

John walked over and stroked along her back. "What is it, girl?" He followed her gaze. Nothing. Silence. His keys must have startled her awake. John pulled her bowls holding water and what remained of her dry food closer to her bed. "You're all set until morning. I'll see you then."

Libbey settled back down and lowered her head, staring up at John with black-onyx eyes.

The night was warm and calm as John exited the garage from the side door and locked it behind him. Tomorrow would be a good day for racing. What he needed now was something in his stomach and sleep. He would meet Mark at the track an hour or two before the race. Mark had returned to his A&P job but found time to show up and help John for his weekend races.

John started the Buick and rolled onto the road. The diner across the street sat dark and empty, save for the festive, colored glow emanating from the silent jukebox. There was no traffic at this hour; he would be home in ten minutes.

Perhaps the lack of traffic made the car parked two blocks away, with a tarp over its roof and doors, more noticeable. What was the point of throwing a plastic tarp over one's car on the street? People did some strange things. Perhaps they were afraid of flying debris, of rain? A car would suffer more injury from debris in motion than parked on the side of the road. It certainly wasn't about to rain; the night sky was clear as black glass. John pondered as he sleepily and steadily drove toward home.

He turned down one street, then another, and was only minutes away from bed. Exhaustion muddled his mind. Maybe it was a police car under that cover. No, from what he could see of the car, it was an older model Ford, and the police in Pittsburgh didn't drive ... Suddenly a rush of adrenaline mixed with insight made John's eyes open wide. Someone was trying to hide the markings of a racecar. The older model black Ford belonged to Murphy. A sick feeling crept over John as he whirled the Buick into a U-turn and stomped on the gas.

By the time John reached the road leading to the garage, the tarped Ford was gone.

The garage sat dark and silent. Through the glass in the bay doors, the soft, white glow of the bathroom light peeked into the darkness as the Buick screeched to a halt. John ran to the side door from which he had left and was sickened to find it open. He stumbled into the garage, arm flailing along the wall for the switch. Light flooded the garage, forcing John to blink back the brightness to focus. A wave of anger, nausea, and dizziness swept over him at what he saw. Murphy had taken a pipe wrench to the Hudson's windshield, and under the hood. The hood stood propped open; the dual carburetors had been beaten to a pulp. A twenty-four-inch red wrench lay next to the car.

John took a few steps toward his maimed racer and saw the black shape sprawled on the ground behind the rear fender. He ran and fell to the horrid sight of Libbey, her head moist and red, her tongue protruding from her open mouth, lying motionless in her own blood.

"Nooo!" John screamed as he grabbed at her limp body, drawing it onto his lap and rocking back and forth, the sobs escaping freely. "Not Libbey, not you." He surveyed her wounded head. One blow was all, one blow over her eyes. There was no fresh blood coming from the wound. He stroked along her blanket-soft fur, along the splash of butterscotch brown on her chest and legs. She was still warm. Now quieted, he rested his hand over her heart, then his head.

There it was, faint but evident. She was still alive.

John stood to one side as the police officers entered and surveyed the damage.

"Hey, Roy, over here," the younger officer called his partner as he squatted next to Libbey. Roy, a taller officer with graying hair and a stern face punctuated with steel blue eyes, stood over the scene and shook his head.

"The car's bad enough, but this is pretty damn low." Turning to John he finished, "Where's your phone?"

John led Officer Roy to the front office and stood silently listening as he dialed the phone and spoke to a muffled voice on the other end of the receiver.

"Say, Doc, it's Sergeant Miller. Listen, I hate to wake you but we've got a situation here. Yep. Rottweiler with a wrench taken to its head. The owner's here; was a break in.

Can you come? Good. We're at Pop's Garage. You know the one, across from the diner. Yep."

The phone clicked and the sergeant looked intently at John, who was trying to take everything in despite his state of shock. "That was an emergency vet we rely on in cases such as this. He runs a clinic out of his farmhouse and will take your dog there tonight. He'll be here in about a half hour. In the meantime, we'll take any information you have."

While keeping a watchful eye on Libbey, John told the officers about seeing Murphy's car parked just a few blocks from the garage but not realizing what it was right away. He told them how Murphy had come to the shop in the past and seemed to be staking it out. The officers put the wrench in a plastic bag to take back to the station for fingerprinting, but they reminded John that most criminals were at least smart enough to wear gloves. John also knew that all he had to go on was circumstantial evidence. The car was covered so he could not prove that it was, indeed, Murphy's Ford. He had not seen Murphy himself. Yet John knew without a doubt what had happened. Murphy probably was liquored up and bragging to his crew how he'd keep Powerhouse from competing the next day, how he was tired of kissing that Hornet's rear and would fix it once and for all.

The vet arrived to find Libbey conscious but weak and whimpering in pain. John had tied a clean cloth around her head and moved her, with the officer's help, to her bed. The vet scribbled his address and phone number on a piece of paper and shoved it into John's hand.

"Call me tomorrow. I'll know more about her prognosis then." He brought a stretcher from the back of his sedan and John helped him lift the one-hundred-twenty-pound dog onto it.

How will I tell Pop without giving him another stroke?

"Please," John said, "do everything you can for her." The man nodded, hopped into his car, and sped off.

The officers retired and John was left alone to clean up the mess. He swept the broken class and mopped the floor where Libbey had lain. It had never dawned on him to see if there had been damage to the customer's car parked in the adjacent bay. He looked now; it was fine. Why shouldn't it be? Murphy wasn't performing random destruction. He didn't even bother to rob the place.

John took a last glance over the garage before heading out. That's when he noticed it. A wry smile crept over his tired face. Tucked in the back corner, hiding under a dirty, white tarp, was the little, white coupe, the original number 23. John slipped the tarp off her smooth curves and sighed. He would be racing tomorrow after all.

John was glad for the two o'clock start time and the close proximity of the Heidelberg track to his home. He managed just five hours sleep before the daylight and his crying son woke him. After a hurried breakfast, he found the slip of paper from the vet and dialed the number. Libbey had suffered internal head injury and a loss of blood. Fortunately, her skull had not been fractured. The doctor had stitched up her wound and watched her through the night for signs of brain swelling. She would survive, but the long-term effects of the injury were uncertain. Here eyesight may be impaired. Now she was resting, and it was recommended that she stay with the doctor and his wife for at least another week for observation. John agreed and thanked the man profusely for what he had done, telling him where to send his bill.

His next call was to Pop. He didn't want a panic if Pop went to the shop and found Libbey missing.

"Hey, Powerhouse, run over any tombstones lately?" It probably had been that long since John had phoned Pop at home in the morning.

"No, Pop. Listen, I have something to tell you."

John slowly, deliberately, explained what had happened from the time he left the garage at 1:00 a.m. to his call to the vet that morning. Pop was silent; not even his breathing could be heard through the phone. "Pop, are you okay? Are you still there?"

"Yeah, yeah." More silence. John just held the phone to his ear and waited.

"What's the vet's phone number? I'm going to go see her."

"That would be a good thing to do."

John arrived at the garage early to make sure the coupe was ready to race. All he had time for was to replace the battery, check the fluids, top off the tires and the gas, and get on the road. He arrived at the track only a half hour prior to the green flag and had to make sure the officials would accept his exchange of car. He explained that the Hudson was "not drivable" at the moment due to engine damage and they hurriedly allowed him to move into third from the pole where he had qualified just two days prior. They knew what was good for them. John had a reputation of putting on a good show and had developed a following. His driving was strong and aggressive. There would have been a lot of upset fans that afternoon if officials had disqualified him from the race.

Mark was anxious and confused about John's late arrival in the coupe.

John answered his questions before he had time to ask them. "Murphy broke into the shop last night and mangled the Hudson," he explained.

Mark was literally speechless, his jaw dropping at the thought that real people did such things.

John noticed Murphy's car in eighth place. No wonder he felt threatened. He was slipping, losing his game. Yet it made the events of last night more unbelievable, more devious. John knew desperate drivers tinkered with an opponent's car before a race when they were close in ability and standing. Murphy was five places back for this average race with only a modest purse. What did he really have to gain from destroying the Hudson other than satisfaction?

An extra dose of adrenaline tinged with hate fueled John and would mark how he drove the coupe. John knew her best, his old friend, and she responded to his every touch as if an extension of his own body. The race was not half complete, and he had lapped first place. He prodded and passed and picked his way past the other cars unceasingly and won a full two miles ahead. These homegrown races were beginning to bore him.

The spectators were exuberant when John smiled up at them and waved. His string of successes had taught him how to work it: flash a toothy smile, make eye contact, make love to the crowd. His energy could pull every Joe in the stands down to victory lane where, just for a moment, they were part of his glory, could feel the speed-high that John possessed, his confidence, and his youth.

An official handed him a small, gold trophy for first place, and the crowd burst with pride. John kissed his prize and held it over his head, until a particular member caught his eye. Along the fringe of bodies standing trackside was a teenage boy, his lank and twisted body confined by a wheelchair. The young man was cheering, but he was unable to clap with the others. His hands were loose and hung from his wrists like pale, wilted roses. John impulsively approached the boy and thrust his trophy into his thin arms, squeezed his shoulders, and backed away.

The shocked teen stared blankly for a moment before breaking into riotous laughter. His friend, manning the wheelchair, gave John an appreciative nod. John was not certain what prompted his gift, other than the boy seemed to deserve it more than he.

"Thank you! Thank you!" the teenager repeated, a wash of emotion caressing his face.

After the crowd had settled and finally left, John pocketed his winnings and turned toward the dried and dusty dirt path leading to his waiting coupe. Several drivers and a few fans still lingered near the track.

"Hey, kid, where's your real car?" Murphy taunted.

John was amazed that Murphy had the guts to ask, given where he'd placed at the end of the day. He seethed and refused to respond. Murphy persisted, confrontational. "I asked you a question, Powers."

John stopped but did not turn to face Murphy, waiting, waiting for him to approach. The muscles in his chest and arms tightened, his hands wadded into a fist. As soon as

Murphy came within reach, John swung around and fired a punch to his face, then another, and another. Murphy, startled, fell back and then retaliated, ramming his fist into John's gut. It only intensified John's anger and he pounded Murphy's face again, sending him reeling into the fence.

John took advantage of the moment and railed into Murphy with blow after blow until his opponent was on the ground stunned and bleeding, unable to respond to the rage assailed on him.

Three men ran to Murphy's aid and grabbed at John's arms in an attempt to pull him away. Before they succeeded, John threw a kick at Murphy's ribcage.

"That's for Libbey!" he yelled.

Chapter Fourteen

HEIDELBERG WAS WASHED OUT. John had shown up with the Hudson ready to dance, but the track was unable to comply. Torrents of rain the night before had left the track a mud hole, and it would be hours before the earth could swallow enough to make the turns manageable. Thick, gray clouds sat overhead, and the air still hung with moisture. John had sent Mark and two teenagers he had brought with him for pit training home and was considering doing the same. Lingering at the track for a while wouldn't hurt. He preferred being here to home. He felt more comfortable, more himself, around the drivers, mechanics, and other aficionados of speed.

He lit a cigarette and leaned against the Hudson as dejected fans began to leave. John had taken up the habit last winter while waiting for the 1955 racing season to commence. He found smoking steadied his hand, calmed him down before a race.

"Hey, sweetness." The sound of her upbeat, friendly voice lifted his mood. Maggie approached and rested a warm hand on his arm. John flicked his cigarette away. It had been too long, and she looked incredible. A sapphire-blue sweater embraced her figure, taunting John to touch. "I came here to see a handsome man win another race. Now what?"

John gazed down at her lovely face, her eyes penetrating into his, and smiled. "What did you have in mind?" He watched as her face glowed with youthful excitement.

"How about a ride? I've always wanted to ride in a racecar."

Moments later, John and Maggie pulled onto the highway in number 23.

"Does it feel strange," Maggie asked, "driving this car at legal speed?"

"Not really. Being on the track triggers my speed response. I can control it on the road."

"Too bad." Maggie slumped in her seat and playfully glanced at the speedometer and then at John, who took the hint.

Peeking in his mirror to ensure there were no police, he floored it, and the Hudson roared down the highway, pushing the needle past one hundred miles per hour. They came upon a car and swerved around it like melted butter falling off a hotcake, then another. Maggie squealed with delight and drew her feet up on the seat, wrapping her arms around her knees.

"Too fast for you?" John yelled.

"No, no, keep going!"

John drove farther, to the edge of the storm clouds where rays of sun poked pencils of misty light earthward. He took the Hudson along an exit ramp and onto a dirt road that was deserted except for a silo and barn on its fringe. The tires bit into the moist dirt, kicking gravel skyward, as John kept up the pace. A mile, then two, passed by in an instant. The Hudson flew over a swell in the road and for a brief moment was airborne, landing at the base with a *chunk*, splashing mud almost to the windows and bouncing John and Maggie inches above their seats. John glanced at Maggie, her eyes wide, and both burst into riotous laughter.

A few miles farther, John slowed to a stop until they could compose themselves.

"My turn." Maggie grabbed the wheel and inched next to John.

He looked at her pensively. "Ah … I don't know."

Maggie pushed her body against John in an attempt to move him, but was not strong enough. "I just want to drive, silly. I won't go as fast as you. We'll save that for the professionals. Now, move over."

John opened the car door and slid out to experience something new, filling the passenger seat in his own racecar. Helen wouldn't even come see him race. This woman was pushing him out of his seat so she could take the wheel.

Maggie turned about and headed back toward the highway, smiling like a kid on too much sugar. John rested his arm along the seat and behind her shoulders. He didn't like handing over control of his own car.

"Do you know where you're going?" he chided.

"Precisely."

"Let me guess: the car wash."

"No!" Maggie laughed.

"The garage to fix my shocks after that jump." Maggie shook her head. "Shopping? The library? I know, back to the track."

"Absolutely not. It's a surprise."

John settled in his seat and gave in. That's what he loved about Maggie. She was full of surprises.

John was taken aback when Maggie drove through town, pulled into the driveway of a sprawling ranch, and parked. She fumbled in her handbag for her house key.

"Bob out of town?" The last thing John needed was another fistfight.

"Uh huh. Permanently. We divorced last fall, John. Come on in and I'll tell you all about it over dinner. You must be starved."

He followed her into the home and found it quite different from his own. Hers was full of color and contemporary style. A dress mannequin modeled a partially completed floral print number in the corner, and John approached for a closer look.

"That's one of my own designs," Maggie chimed.

"For your shop?"

"Don't have the shop just yet. I take customers here at the house or make appointments at their home. I mostly sew from patterns, but for really special occasions, I can design something unique just for them. That one is for a garden party hosted by the mayor's wife."

"Really?" John was impressed. "How do you secure such affluent clients?"

Maggie sighed. "It hasn't been easy. I started by creating a dress for myself—a deep blue brocade—and wearing it to the theater, opera, charitable events, anything I could attend where there would be money. I was at a performance of *A Midsummer Night's Dream* and met a woman in the powder room during intermission. She commented on my dress, and I handed her a card. Amazingly enough, her daughter was getting married and she hired me to make dresses for her three attendants. It's been word of mouth since then."

"You have talent."

"Thanks. My talent was the beginning of the end with Bob." Maggie walked into the kitchen and John followed. "He came home one Friday from his out-of-town office and saw me all dressed up, heading out for the theater. Well, he immediately assumed I was going to meet a man. I offered him to come along and see for himself, but he just blew up and refused to listen. Is chicken all right?"

"Sure." John watched Maggie bustle around her kitchen, putting a pan of water on the stove. "What can I do?"

Maggie seemed surprised that he would ask. "Oh, here," she said while setting several potatoes and a bunch of carrots on the counter next to the sink. "You can peel these and put them in the pot. Or you can set the table if you like. The plates are here." She touched the cupboard. "Silverware's in that drawer."

John got to work.

"So, Bob?" he continued.

"He really made me angry that evening when he refused to believe me. Every day he treated me as if I were cheating on him, making terrible comments. I was convinced that he wanted our marriage to be over and was looking for something to use against me so he could move forward with his plan."

Maggie cleaned the chicken, brushed it with melted butter, and sprinkled it with salt and pepper, her hands working quickly as she spoke. "I was relieved when he had to leave for work two weeks later. While he was gone, I confided in one of my customers who saw that I was down. She convinced me to have Bob followed."

"You hired a detective!" John laughed and tossed the spuds into the waiting pot.

"Yes, and I'm glad I did. My hunch was right. He had been having an affair with a woman in Chicago for three years. Three years! Do you know he actually offered to marry her? With me sitting here keeping his home and waiting for him to show up and play husband. Incredible." Maggie shook her head as she pushed the roasting pan full of chicken into the oven. "He didn't even wait for us to be through before he tried to marry someone else. I'm glad he's gone. Now I can focus on my career."

Done with her preparations, Maggie stood watching John set forks on the table. "You know," she started, "I actually feel more confident now that I'm not relying to Bob to make me feel like a complete woman. It does get a bit lonely at times though. When Bob was here, there was someone in the house at least."

"Well, you've got some company now."

Maggie smirked. "Yes, I sort of corralled you, didn't I?" She looked knowingly at his face, silently leaning against the kitchen counter.

John caught her gaze. He didn't mind being here. Maggie was comfort. He felt more relaxed and at home in her presence than he ever had with Helen. Maggie let him just be. The peace of it, the centeredness of not feeling guilty about his racing, was soothing and exhilarating. Maggie seemed to pick up his thoughts.

"I know you're married now, John. Since the divorce, I've been snooping where you're concerned and actually saw your little family at the grocers just before Christmas. Helen is beautiful, John, and the babies!" She rolled her eyes for emphasis. "Just precious. Your wife was buying a ham and all the trimmings—she seemed very happy that day." Maggie gave a nervous little laugh, caught her voice, and looked away.

John thought he saw her eyes mist. "Helen likes the winter months because I'm home and not racing."

"She doesn't approve of your racing?"

John shook his head. "She hates it actually. She's convinced I'm going to end up dead, or at least maimed, and refuses to come to a race. Then there's the lack of consistent income … though I can earn decent winnings, which is pretty often."

"It is a dangerous sport; she has a right to worry."

John opened his mouth to protest.

"However," Maggie continued, "we can't spend our days in fear, afraid of the very thing that gives us purpose, can we? Look at me. It would have been so easy to apply for the steno pool at the university or ring up groceries for a living instead of creating expensive dresses and trying to convince women to spend their husbands' money on them. I don't know. Some days I still wonder if I'm doing the right thing. It would kill me not to."

John agreed. Yes, it would kill him not to race. Kill his spirit, his sense of adventure, his joy. Maggie understood. Why was it so impossible for Helen to grasp?

"I hope this won't be a problem—you're having a little dinner with an old friend," Maggie said a bit sheepishly.

"No," John answered. "She thinks I'm at the racetrack and won't be home for hours. She won't even miss me. Besides, I don't check in with Helen. We have our own direction and don't tell each other what to do. *At least not out loud*, John thought. In his own ears, John's words sounded like a proposition. *Well, she can take it or leave it.* He hoped she would have the sense to take it.

Maggie turned down the stove and set the oven timer. "Relax for a few moments. I want to freshen up." She popped into the living room and put a Wanda Jackson album on the stereo, then drifted into the far end of the house.

John didn't believe this was an impromptu dinner between casual friends. Maggie had planned it, had hoped he would come home with her after the race, and had probably made a dress for the occasion. He smiled casually. Being pursued by a beautiful, sexy woman was exciting, a slow and calculated exciting, and not like chasing first place. He knew he was already at the checkered flag where Maggie was concerned.

Nearly twenty minutes passed when John heard the music change from boisterous Wanda Jackson to a smooth cascade of strings. Maggie emerged and John held his breath as she slowly approached, dressed in a form-fitting, satiny dress the color of cream and high heels, her hair twisted cleanly up with soft, wispy tendrils framing her forehead.

She held an open bottle in one hand and two glasses in the other.

"A little wine before dinner always helps me relax." Maggie handed the bottle to John and stood close for him to pour, so close that her dress rubbed his arm and the scent of White Shoulders mingled with the fruity blend of chardonnay splashing to the wine goblets.

John rested the bottle on the table and took his glass from Maggie, her lovely face only inches from his. John found her every move absorbing and sensuous; he could not take his eyes from her.

"Shall we toast?" she suggested as she lifted her glass. "To the fulfillment of aspirations."

John smiled and clinked his glass to hers. Each took a sip, eyes fixated on the other. John reached down and took her free hand in his, caressing, studying her fingers. All the years he had known Maggie, he had never allowed himself the pleasure of touching her. Not since that night when, as a teenager still prepping the coupe, they parked in her blue Chevy outside his front door and she had taken his hand to say good night. That night seemed from another reality.

Slowly, tenderly, he leaned forward as his lips found the welcoming softness of hers. His hand found her satin dress.

Maggie drew in a breath and gave a soft, shuddering sigh. "John, I ..." she began to protest.

"Shhhh, it's all right."

"No, John. I love you. I always have."

Chapter Fifteen

Abbottstown Race, Helen

HELEN'S FINGERS TREMBLED AS she gathered the bonnet's pink ribbons under Susan's chin and tied a bow. The baby gurgled and squeezed her Raggedy Ann close. Why should she be nervous? The resolve had come as a sudden break in the clouds after a thunderstorm, a shimmer of sunlight that would change everything. It had taken months—no, years—to talk herself into this place of acceptance. She would douse fear and distrust and refuse to let it ignite. Helen had decided to support her husband in his dream. He had made the NASCAR circuit, and today's race was the only one close enough for her to attend. She planned to show up unannounced to surprise John after the race.

A little smile curved her lips as she studied her children playing together on the floor. Michael was stacking blocks and Susan was gleefully knocking them over. Hadn't Helen been playing the same game? She had been trying to knock John's blocks over, hoping he would give up the game and get on to something else. Now she would step back and watch what he could build.

Dressed more appropriately for Sunday church service than for a NASCAR race, Helen gathered the children and loaded them into the Buick. This was a special day. She wanted them to look festive when John spotted his family in the stands. When they joined him after the race for hugs and kisses, she wanted his heart to swell with pride. Perhaps it was anticipation that made her stomach flip, or the thought of attending a race with the children after so many years of refusing to set foot at the track. A deep breath and the Buick rolled out of the driveway and toward an act that, Helen trusted, would rekindle John's affection. It would take over three hours to reach Lincoln Speedway at Abbottstown.

Clutching Michael's hand, and Susan in the other arm, Helen made her way through the crowd to their seats. Her dress pockets billowed with candy, chewing gum, a sock puppet, and a rattle, anything to keep small children occupied while racecars circled the track for seemingly endless miles. Though only late May, the day was hot and sunny; Susan was already fussing and trying to pull off her bonnet.

"No, baby, you need to keep that on … avoid the sun," Helen said.

They sat about fifty yards left of the pole position, halfway up the bleachers. She scanned the lineup of racecars below; her heart leapt with pride and recognition when she spotted John's 1956 Chevy third from the pole. It was an amazing red and white machine sparkling in the sunshine—the familiar "23" emblazoned on the roof and doors. To Helen, it seemed too beautiful to submit to the rigors and dust of the racetrack. John was fortunate to have a Chevy sponsorship for the NASCAR circuit. They were paying him quite a bit just to race the Bel Air, based on their mind-set of "Win on Sunday; sell on Monday!'

"John!" Helen called out. "John, up here!" but her voice was lost among the noise of the excited crowd anxious for the action to begin.

"Daddy can't hear you," Michael said, his face sad.

"Don't worry. We'll go see Daddy after the race."

Michael was appeased.

A middle-aged couple seated one row below turned to check out the little family. "Are you Mrs. Powers, honey?" the woman asked.

"Yes, yes, I'm John's wife."

"Oh!" the woman's eyes lit up and she rose from her seat, followed by her husband. "Well, aren't you sweet? I have to give you a hug. This is William, and I'm Agnes. We hardly miss a race, and that young man of yours is quite the driver. We just know he will be the pride of NASCAR one day. Everybody is talking about it."

Helen felt ashamed. She had no idea her husband was so celebrated.

The woman's husband finally spoke. "Shouldn't you be sitting with the families? "

"The families?" Helen was at a loss.

"Yes." Agnes pointed toward the pole position. "This track keeps the first few rows open for the driver's families, just over there."

"Oh," Helen stammered, "I didn't know if I'd be able to come until the last minute."

"Well, honey, you enjoy the race with your precious babies, and good luck to you."

Helen thanked the woman and slouched in her seat. Perhaps this wasn't such a good idea. Would she be able to get to John after the race? Would he be embarrassed because she wasn't sitting with the other wives?

She looked into John's car and saw him glancing at the grandstand, into the area Agnes had just pointed out. Was he looking for her? There wasn't time to ruminate as the order of, "Gentlemen, start your engines," blared over the track, followed by a loud growl from the machines below.

Susan, startled by the sudden and very loud noise, broke into a wail. Helen held her close and stroked the soft curls that peeked out from her bonnet and sat against her pink neck. "It's all right, there, there. Watch the pretty red and white car. Daddy's in that one."

Susan took a few moments to settle down. "Daddy!" she exclaimed.

"That's right; we're going to cheer for Daddy to win."

The cars were in motion, following the pace car around the track, while gaining speed. The pace car moved off the track and speed took over. Helen put her hand to her mouth and squeezed her eyes shut as the cars roared past, engines full open. The fumes, the noise, made her nauseous. Her imagination wanted to focus on terrible things. She saw the red and white car spinning out of control, crashing, fire, and explosion. Her stomach turned. *Stop. Stop.* "Stop!" she called aloud to turn off the pictures in her mind, and she was grateful the roaring engines drowned out her voice.

She focused on the smiling, cheering fans surrounding her. *It's fine,* she reasoned. *All of these people wouldn't come here if it was dangerous. Those wives sitting in the special section, they are supportive of what their husbands are doing. This is a sport, not a war. John has accepted the risk of his passion. Shouldn't I?* Helen fixed her gaze on the red and white Chevy hurling down the track, squeezing between the barricade and its contenders, tires spitting rubber at each turn. Her fingers caressed the silver crucifix around her neck. She sent up a prayer for her modern-day gladiator fighting the battle of speed.

One hundred fifty laps passed with John swapping first place twice. The children were settled in, Susan watching her brother roll his red metal car along the seat between them. Helen became mesmerized by the circling cars, by the engine song ringing in her ears, and by the round and round motion. She could not take her eyes off John's car. As he passed below, she could see his profile, stern and intense, behind the wheel. She felt so proud at that moment—proud of John for persisting against anything that stood in his way, even her, to pursue his dream, and proud of herself for forcing past the barrier of fear and resentment. Yes, there had been resentment. John possessed the gumption and freedom to do what his soul commanded without reservation. What would she do if she had such conviction and freedom?

The race continued uneventfully with no cautions, no spinouts, and no lost tires. Helen marveled at the speed and agility of the pit crews when the drivers pulled in for gas or tires. She watched with interest as John pitted the Chevy. It put him back a number of places, but he made them up. Helen was amazed by John's unswerving focus. He was intense and drove aggressively close to the other cars.

His nerve increased during the last twenty laps. Now in third place, he seemed almost desperate to get past the Chrysler blocking his dance with the first place contender. The red and white Chevy skimmed the inside track at the turn and bore down on the white Chrysler. It seemed he would almost make it, but there was not enough room. Helen's breath stopped as she watched John's front bumper approach within inches of the Chrysler, attempting to pass on the left in the narrow space created when the Chrysler moved up. Then the Chevy eased up a bit as if to wait for an opening. A swell of fear rose in her chest and choked her cry as, in the next moment, John pushed the Chevy with everything it had and rammed the rear corner of the Chrysler, sending his challenger spinning out of control in the middle of the track. The Chrysler flipped twice toward the grandstand before settling back on all four tires. Instantly upon impact, the Chevy slid sideways as the rear end caught up with the point of impact.

Helen could make out John fighting with the steering wheel; the Chevy careened briefly then straightened, slipping past the wreckage to chase first place. A moan rose from the crowd and mingled with the sound of squealing tires and groaning metal as racers struggled to career around the dead Chrysler, some coming into contact with its battered white body or with each other as they veered and twisted.

Dust rose from the dirt track, making it hard to see. What was happening?

A yellow flag flailed above the track, slowing the cars in their positions.

"Look!" someone screamed behind her.

Helen glanced down to see flames shooting from the Chrysler's engine compartment. The driver was still inside! Several men ran toward the burning car, one toting a stretcher. The first to arrive tugged at the driver's door, but it wouldn't budge. The driver was coherent but obviously in pain. He yelled something at the men and soon one of them pried the opposite door open and crawled into the car. He grabbed the driver around the chest and tugged. The flames grew, releasing into the stands black smoke that stung her eyes and bathed everything in its stench. *Oh, hurry!*

A few more tugs and the driver was half out of the car. Now able to reach, two others each grabbed around a leg and pulled the driver to the ground. Helen heard the cry of pain as the driver was carried away from the car and toward the grassy middle of the track. A cheer rose from the enthralled crowd. Only moments later, the flames found the gas line and the Chrysler was engulfed.

By now, the slowed racers had made their way around the track and were passing the point of the accident. Helen strained to see John's face as the Chevy passed but was unable to. From her vantage point, John had hit the Chrysler purposely in ambition of a win. Her hands shook from the realization of it.

The intensity on the track over, she turned her attention to the children. Susan was oblivious, still holding her dolly and half dozing. One look at Michael, and Helen was sorry she had come. His face bore a look of worry, his eyes brimming with tears. He was out of his chair, standing silently. What had he seen? How much did he understand?

She pulled his little body toward her and squeezed him close. The touch from his mother made his tears spill over, and he quickly wiped them away. "It's over now. Everyone is all right. See, there's the ambulance to take that man to the hospital where he can be looked after."

"Is he hurt bad, Momma?"

"Oh, I don't think so," Helen lied. "Perhaps he just twisted his ankle and that's why he couldn't hop out of the car by himself."

Satisfied with her answer, Michael managed a small smile.

With a wave of the green flag, the cars sped into action.

Only fourteen laps remained with John and a Dodge riding out the last side by side. Helen held her breath each time John inched forward. He was in a good position to pass at a half car length, yet the other driver was just fast enough to elude him. The two cars wrestled for twelve laps and then John broke away on the third curve, pushing the Dodge up and passing on the left at the inside track, easing his way to first place. The other car was forced to slow just enough for John to take the lead.

My God, Helen thought, *he's going to win this thing.* The red and white Chevy rode full bore around the track, dodging less skilled drivers lagging a lap behind, the Dodge only a few feet from his tail. The white flag shook; Helen's pride swelled with the rising clamor from the stands. The crowd stood in unison to witness the climax.

"Daddy's going to win!" she yelled toward Michael, who was bouncing with pent-up energy. "Daddy's going to win!"

She lifted Susan high to see the pretty car, now covered with dust, forge over the finish line in first place. Helen didn't know how to control the surge of emotion coursing through her—shock, exhilaration, pride, and a touch of fear. What should she do now? She watched as John took an extra lap then came to the front and spun a few doughnuts before parking the Chevy and hopping out of the car, his arms raised in glory before throngs of cheering admirers. It was all too much.

"You need to go down," Agnes was coaching her. "Go down to be with your husband for the presentation of the trophy and photos."

"Yes, thank you." Helen took Michael's hand and started inching past spectators. "Nice to have met you," she hollered at the couple as she began descending the steps.

She spotted John's smiling face below. He was being interviewed by someone with a microphone, but the sound did not reach into the stands. *John is so handsome when he smiles,* Helen thought with the realization that she had not seen him smile in a long time. If only she could move faster! People were milling about and cluttering the steps down to the track. How excited he would be to see her and the children.

There was the trophy glimmering in the sun. John held it against his chest as a photographer's camera snapped images of what was probably the highlight of John's life to this moment. Helen found an empty row of seats that would allow her to cut across toward the finish line, above the crowd that had gathered below. She guided Michael into the row, still holding Susan on one hip. Perhaps John could hear her now. She released Michael's hand and cupped her hand around her mouth to amplify her voice. *"Joh … n."*

What she saw next stopped the word in her throat. An attractive blonde woman in a blue dress had emerged from the crowd. She ran up to John, wrapped her arms around him, and kissed him on the mouth. Not the quick peck of a stranger overtaken with admiration but a passionate kiss. Helen's mind whirled with explanations. She's just an excited fan. John probably hates being mauled by strangers.

"We have to hurry," Helen coaxed Michael as he nodded and placed his small hand in hers. Yet, as the three approached, Helen saw John place his arm around the woman's shoulder. She saw her turn to face the reporters and cameras, smiling brightly, beaming with pride. This strange, lovely woman stood with John, her hand resting on his as it draped over her shoulder. John smiled and continued his conversation with the reporter as people began pressing in toward the pair.

Helen's stomach fell to her shoes as she watched John lean toward the woman and return her kiss, then he lifted his trophy high among cheers and clicking cameras. The crowd slowly engulfed John until Helen could no longer see him. Her heart felt like putty; she could barely breathe.

Scooping up Michael in her free arm, she hurriedly made her way toward the exit, hoping her babies were not alarmed by the tears streaming down her face.

Chapter Sixteen

Abbottstown Race, John

JOHN SQUINTED AGAINST THE sun to survey the track on this hot race day in late May and wondered why he had never raced in Abbottstown before. Lincoln Speedway was only about three hours from Pittsburgh and had recently been added to the NASCAR Grand National circuit. The sun sparkled off the Chevy's polished metal and warmed the red steering wheel under his grasp. A momentary flashback to a cherry-red racer atop derby hill many summers earlier brought a smile. He had lost focus that day, and it cost him. John slid the goggles over his eyes and adjusted his helmet strap. This time, he had every reason to anticipate a win. The new 1956 sport coupe parked third from the pole had given him a good early season and made his sponsors happy. He was concerned about keeping Chevrolet and Pure Oil happy, as he needed their support to stay in NASCAR. He had broken free of the weekend hobbyists at the local tracks and found traveling the South and running new tracks packed with thousands of fans exhilarating. He could never go back.

A good crowd had shown up and was making plenty of racket. John briefly glanced toward the grandstand and into the closest section to the pole. There sat his loveliest supporter wearing her trademark blue. Maggie loved to watch him race, was excited when he placed well, and begged to accompany him on out-of-town trips. He had felt a rush of excitement and anticipation when collecting her on the way to the Daytona Beach race in February. The pair didn't return until after the Palm Beach race on March 4. He didn't have to worry about Helen showing up—even at the local races such as this one. She would rather be caught dead than at a car race and had told him as much, many times. She "didn't want to be there when he got hurt or killed," she had said, as if it were a certainty. Her pervasive negative attitude toward what he craved, what he *was*, gnawed away at any affection he once felt for Helen. Their marriage had become stiff and formal, his home simply a stopping place between races where he dropped off the better part of his pay. As far as his NASCAR friends knew, he was single and dating a gorgeous blond named Maggie. Even Helen seemed oblivious to his change of heart.

John snapped into the present at the call of "Gentlemen, start your engines." The small-block V-8 rumbled and growled under the hood. John felt a surge of joy pulse through him, followed by a thin veil of sadness—like an afterthought. In the course of a moment, he experienced an overwhelming sense of continuity with everyone he had ever known—with every incident of his life. It was unlike anything he had sensed before, and the feeling almost overwhelmed him. He sucked air into his lungs in an effort to alleviate the strange sensation, the congruence of time and place that settled on him like fog. Then, before the green flag had waved, the sensation was gone. It seemed several minutes had passed, but it had been only a few seconds. Weird. Was he going to die on the track today? *Don't even think it. Push it away and focus, dammit. Focus.*

The race was underway. Nothing existed except the track, the contenders, and an expert driver cloaked in a red and white Bel Air.

Near the end of the race, John was frustrated. There were only thirty laps to go, and he had spent much of the race picking his way back to third after a pit stop landed him in fifth place. Now he was wrestling a white Chrysler sitting in second. The driver seemed to know John's strategy and did all he could to keep the Chevy squarely behind. John rode so close to the Chrysler that it looked as if he were pushing it along. Yet the Chrysler was just a little faster. John couldn't push him out of the way or get around him. Forced to slow at each turn, John backed off as the Chrysler held tightly on the track and kept just enough ahead to beat John to the inside. John would have to try a new strategy. With only twenty laps to go, he needed to do something *now*.

Curve four approached—John held a groove under the Chrysler and gunned the engine coming out of the turn. His fresh tires grabbed the dirt, and the Chevy made it down the track before the Chrysler. Not by enough. He failed to hold a position beside the Chrysler. The Chevy's right front fender lined up with the Chrysler's left taillight less than a foot behind. The Chrysler would move back down, John reasoned, blocking his Chevy yet again. He wouldn't let it happen. He had had enough. John eased back just enough on the gas to create some space, as if setting up a pool shot, then angrily mashed the pedal, ramming the Chrysler's rear corner. The result was an impact with enough velocity to send the Chrysler reeling. It flipped twice and hit the barricade fence separating the track from the spectators. John wrenched the steering wheel to straighten the Chevy after impact and was able to sail around the Chrysler.

The yellow flag emerged and John slowed, planning his strategy to overtake the Dodge riding in first place. There were still enough laps to get him there. The Chrysler was on fire … John glanced from the track just long enough to survey the accident scene. Good, they were carrying the driver safely away. *Oh, my God!* The Chrysler was swallowed by flames and thick, black, putrid smoke charged into the air. *That must be it,* John considered, *the reason for the weird feeling I had earlier.* He was close to the action, but tragedy had been averted and all he knew now was that he was a car length from winning. The green flag flailed over the track, and John moved in for the kill.

John pulled into the drive at just after 2:00 a.m. He quietly turned the key in the lock. Given the post-race festivities, he was tired but still worked up. He was surprised to find the kitchen lit and Helen sitting fully dressed at the table. Her face was red and puffy, her hair disheveled. *Here it comes,* John mulled. *She's angry because I'm not home by curfew.*

"What's wrong?" John asked.

Helen's look was filled with exasperation and disgust. She shoved several handwritten pages across the table at her husband.

"While I've been sitting here waiting for you, I decided to write it down. It's all there; read it."

John picked up the pages casually and glanced at the writing scrawled between the lines. "First let me say, I have loved you very much," it read.

He continued through the first paragraph, until reaching the line that read, "So, I decided to surprise you by attending the race in Abbottstown."

John dropped the papers on the table. "You were there?"

"Yes, I was there; and so were your children." Helen's voice shook.

"Why didn't you tell me you wanted to see the race? I could have taken you there myself, made arrangements for—"

"Arrangements for your girlfriend to stay home! How long have you been with her, John, how long?"

John's shoulders dropped. There was no point in holding back now. "I've known Maggie since I was fifteen, since before we met, though she was married then and was always just a friend. I didn't even know where she lived. A year ago she divorced and showed up at Heidelberg after a race."

Helen listened, her eyes fixed on John's face, cold and empty. "Have you slept with her?" When John would not respond, she slammed her fist on the table and yelled the same words into his stunned face. "Have you slept with her, John?"

"Yes! Yes, I have—many times. What do you expect? She supports what I do, she shows up. My God, Helen, she's been more of a wife to me than you ever were."

Helen closed her eyes and shook her head against John's bitter words.

"Well, that's all that really matters, isn't it? Being there for you at the racetrack. Forget raising your kids, keeping your house, holding things together so you have someplace to call home. Everything has always revolved around you and your racing! Well, here's a news flash for you, John Powers: you have been a pretty lousy husband." Helen's voice elevated. "Disappearing when your son was born, leaving me with a baby and no money so you could chase your precious pastime."

"Sure, go ahead, rub it in my face. I'm a selfish bastard because I didn't settle for a normal job. Here, you want to see if it's been worth it?" John pulled a wad of hundred dollar bills from his pocket and threw it on the table. "You want money, you've got it."

"I don't want money. I want a marriage. I want a father for our kids."

"What does that mean? You're not happy unless I'm unhappy. You're only satisfied when I'm stuck at some job I hate and limited to racing as a hobby when it's convenient for you. I've made it to NASCAR, and that means being out of town, it means sporadic income, and it means I'm doing exactly what I've spent my life chasing!"

The raised voices woke Susan; her wails penetrated the walls. Soon, Michael joined in.

Helen stood and pushed her letter toward John. "I'm tired. You can do whatever you want, John, but our marriage is done. I won't divorce you until I know Michael and Susan will be financially cared for, until I can support them on my own, but our relationship is over."

"It's been over," John responded coolly.

He watched Helen slowly ascend the stairs to tend to the children. He sat in the kitchen until he heard Helen draw a bath, then he went upstairs and pulled a suitcase from the closet, quickly packed everything he would need for the next few days, and walked out the front door. Helen's letter sat unread where she had left it.

Chapter Seventeen

"**WHAT WILL YOU DO?**" Pop handed the letter back to John. He had just read that the corporate sponsors of John's team were pulling their support. The 1964 season had been rough. Three drivers had been killed: Joe Weatherly, Fireball Roberts, and Jimmy Purdue. The white collars were getting squeamish.

"We'll have to find new sponsors. It reminds me of when the auto companies pulled their NASCAR backing in '57. Remember? That ended up being a good time to be in NASCAR. The new promoters paid higher winnings to entice the drivers and owners to stay." Even the auto companies had succumbed to fear and the bad press that had raged after an incident at Martinsville Speedway in

Virginia resulted in five spectators being hurt, including an eight-year-old boy.

Pop refilled his coffee cup and returned to his seat. The garage wouldn't open for another hour and the two were alone on this chill October morning. John preferred this time of day at the shop. Surrounded by the smell of rubber, oil and thick coffee, John enjoyed the quiet interrupted only by Pops familiar voice. Being here, just the two men, took John back to the days of building a cherry-red racer in the corner as his mentor healed sick cars. He could not allow himself to become lost in nostalgia now. Otherwise, he would not be able to make his pitch.

"I've been thinking," he began, "of selling my ownership share in the garage."

Pop gulped at his hot coffee. "Really? Why?"

"Maggie and I are talking about moving. The travel and time away during the race season is starting to get to her. We thought if we moved south, closer to the circuit, it might ease up a bit. Now is a good time to look for a place. We want to be settled before the race season starts." John watched Pop's face for a reaction. He wasn't just leaving the garage; he would be leaving Pittsburgh. Pop showed no emotion, his features taught. "After all, since Helen moved the kids to Chicago six years ago, there has been nothing to hold me here." Once he said the words, John wished he hadn't. Pop might think he was brushing him off, that it would not tear him up leaving behind the best friend a guy could have. No, Pop would know better. John needed to leave; to start fresh and forget about the years he spent struggling his way toward a full-time racing career.

Pop sighed, and John saw the weariness that settled around his eyes and pulled at the corners of his mouth. "I'd like to buy you out, but I'm not able to right now."

It was true that Pop's Garage had increased in value since John had joined the NASCAR circuit. Though John was rarely present at the shop, he had dumped considerable funds into upgrading equipment and adding more bays as the property would permit. John's affiliation with the garage was the best marketing tool Pop ever had. A team of seven mechanics managed the work, and customers were willing to wait weeks for an appointment for less urgent repairs.

"Would you consider another partner? I can find someone to buy my share."

"No. I'm too old to start with a new partner." Pop leaned forward and stared into his black coffee as if an answer could be extracted from it. "I've been putting this off for a few years now. Suppose I didn't want to think about it, but it's obviously time." John looked confused. "I'll sell the shop outright and go into retirement," Pop continued.

"Is that what you want?"

"Many years from now, you will learn it's not always possible to keep up with what one wants."

"What do you mean? You're doing fine."

"No, I'm not. I'm past seventy, lame from a stroke, and can't keep up with the work."

"What about Smitty and the other mechanics? They do most of the repairs." Even though he said it, John knew that Pop was unable to keep himself away from the day-to-day workings of the shop. He could never relegate himself to scheduling appointments and ordering parts. Getting his hands on the guts of a car was Pop's life. It was all he knew.

Pop moved to the seat next to his young friend and draped his arm across John's shoulders. "We've run this place together for a long time, Powerhouse. It's been a nice ride, but it's time to stop. You've done it! You made it to the NASCAR Grand Nationals. You can't stay here. It would never be the same with someone else, and I'd rather turn the whole lot over to someone with the stamina and ideas to keep its reputation up."

John could understand that, logically. He had a harder time imagining anyone else running Pop's Garage. Just the thought of it seemed like death, like an end to his childhood memories, of his first racecar, of learning how to handle a track in Pop's Olds. In a perfect world, Pop would always be standing at the doorway to his shop, sporting a conductor's cap, a red bandana poking from the bib of his overalls, and a bright smile on his tanned face, waving as John and number 23 rode off into the sunset. To John, who was moving on with his new wife to live out his racing career, that is how he would always remember home.

Chapter Eighteen

JOHN WAS SURE THIS was a bad idea. He would wait just ten minutes more until he was out of there. Why would Michael have picked this place, a family restaurant dripping with mauve and green floral print everywhere he looked? Perhaps its proximity to the airport was the reason. Michael had said he would only be in town for one day. The food had better be good. He knew of several places in North Carolina where he could have at least ordered a few beers before dinner. He wished Maggie had come along. When his son phoned several weeks ago asking to meet John for dinner, she insisted that he go alone. Never mind that he hadn't seen the kid in twenty-two years, ever since his mother moved them to Chicago in '58.

According to John, it could only mean one thing. Michael had probably been following his racing career and wanted money. John had done quite well for himself since leaving Pennsylvania and moving south in the late '60s to be closer to the NASCAR circuit. Between Maggie's design firm and his racing, the two of them bought the best house money could buy in North Carolina. Of course, Maggie was sentimental about leaving the Pittsburgh area. "It's where we met, where our roots are," she had said. She recently convinced John to buy a condominium near Pittsburg where they could visit the old haunts and reminisce.

Their first trip back to the area was a disappointment. So much had changed. Heidelberg was gone. Pop never did sell the garage. A few buyers showed interest, yet Pop was not able to hand over his baby. The garage had been torn down by the mid '70s and was eventually replaced by a strip mall. The diner across the street was still in business but seemed run down and dingy, not the sparkling clean center of activity from his youth. Pocono was the nearest track, and it was located several hours from Pittsburgh. The new speedways were much larger, paved, and catered more to the fans than their predecessors.

Now in his forties, John was twice the age of some of the young bucks populating the track and had made a strong presence in the world of racing—so different from when he first cut his teeth on the dirt tracks near Pittsburgh. The moment he sensed himself slowing down, he would retire. John Powers planned to go out swiftly and suddenly before he really became the old man of the track.

John pouted over his soft drink and did not notice someone approach his table.

"John Powers?" John looked up and knew the man standing before him was his son. Thick, dark hair and blue eyes, tall, the kid was good looking. John stood. Michael stood just a few inches taller. He had worn a suit and tie for the occasion. John almost felt intimidated until he realized Michael was nervous. Probably why he was late, he had to work up the courage to face a father he barely remembered.

The two men locked hands in a brief acknowledgment and sat.

"You look good," John started. "What have you been doing with yourself?" That sounded idiotic. What else did you say to someone you haven't seen since he was in kindergarten?

"Thanks. Let's see, I started in a law practice after graduation and have been married two years. April and I have a little girl: Samantha." Michael pulled his wallet from his pocket and flipped it open to reveal a photo of a petite brunette, apparently April, holding a baby in a christening dress.

"Hmmm. A lawyer you say? You enjoy that sort of thing?"

"Yes, yes I do. I'm a defense attorney and find my work very rewarding."

"Helen must be proud."

The waitress arrived and took their order. John was curious about this young man, his voice almost identical to his own, his face similar, yet his tone and mannerisms much different from his own.

Michael shifted the conversation quickly away from himself. "Susan's doing well. She just finished nursing school last summer and is working at the hospital pediatrics unit. She says she loves it."

John felt almost put off, yet vaguely pleased, that his offspring had done so well in his absence. Helen made sure they acquired what she had not: a college education while still young and before family came along. Though he had supported Helen financially those first few years after the break-up and had paid child support thereafter, he knew she struggled with working full time, raising the kids, and taking classes for her business degree.

"How's your mother?"

"That's actually why I called you here. Momma is pretty sick. She had cancer eight years ago and went through a mastectomy, chemo, and the whole gamut of treatments. She did great for a long time. We thought it was gone, but she contracted lymphoma and the cancer is spreading quickly. She won't survive the summer."

"What do you want from me?" John said.

"Momma's been asking for you. She wants to see you before, well, before she dies." The younger man's hands rested on the table, fingers intertwined, loosened, and then came together again. His eyes became sad as he spoke of his mother. He calmed, almost to the point of looking tired, and stared intently at John's face, waiting for a response.

John was surprised that Helen would have any interest in seeing him. "Didn't Helen remarry?"

"She's had a few men show interest over the years but couldn't bring herself to marry again." Michael seemed uncomfortable by his own statement and looked away.

The food arrived, but he was not eating. For a moment, John felt sorry for him. They must be struggling to handle her medical bills, he reasoned. Michael with a new career and young family, Susan just starting out. Why else would he have called an outsider who was removed from his life for over two decades and flown all the way from Chicago to see him? John knew that Helen would not want to see him now. Frankly, they were all strangers to him, and he did not want to get involved. He would offer financial assistance and nothing more.

"If it will help, I can loan you some cash for Helen's medical bills."

Michael shook his head. "No, that's not it. We don't want any money. Momma wants to talk to you. I think … I think she wants to make peace, to tell you that she forgives you."

"Forgives me?" John was insulted, "for what? For having a relationship with someone who happened to support me, who, by the way, has supported me all these years? Helen and I could have worked it out. We could have stayed together if your mother had really wanted to. She turned it off so fast it would make your head spin. You know why? Because she never wanted to be married to me in the first place! I was never good enough for her and her doctor father."

Michael stared blankly back, stunned into silence. After a few moments, he spoke, his voice smooth and words deliberate. "Look, I don't expect you to want any involvement in our lives. Between you and me, it took everything I had to come here today and face you, to ask you for anything. I would just as soon never lay eyes on you. I came here for Momma, because it's what she wants. The woman is dying. Can't you see beyond yourself to respect that?"

John glared at his son. He didn't need a guilt trip laid on him and refused to own it. He had done what was expected of him by providing financial support. As far as he was concerned, Helen made her decision the night of the Abbottstown race when she told him the marriage was over. If she needed to rehash the past now, well, that was her own concern.

"I'm sorry, I can't help."

Michael leaned back in his chair, a look of incredulity on his face. He motioned for the server to bring the bill. "You know, I expected nothing less."

"How would you know what to expect? You don't know me."

"Mr. Powers, I don't care to know you." Michael snatched up the bill and reached into his suit coat pocket, pulling from it a paper folded to the size of a postcard and worn around the edges. "Momma told me you probably wouldn't come so to give you this. You may want to read it this time." He tossed the paper on the table.

John glanced at it and sat motionless.

"Pick it up," Michael commanded.

John lifted the letter and stuffed it in his shirt pocket as if it were no more than a used napkin. Michael turned and walked from the restaurant. John watched him until out of sight. He knew it would be the last time he would lay eyes on his son.

John ate his dinner in thoughtful silence, remembering, wondering. He pulled the letter from his pocket and began to unfold it, then recognized what it was and returned it. Old news. He might read it later out of modest curiosity, to see what she had written on the night he left. Whatever it said, it told a story of long ago that no longer mattered, a story of one day in the history of his career on a barely known track in Pennsylvania, a day on which the rest of his life pivoted. John's need to win moved into a darker place at that race and he would do whatever it took. Winning it gave him a cocky sense of self that refused to compromise. Staying with Helen would have been too much work just to get to a place he already knew with Maggie. Once John Powers made up his mind, there was no turning back. He found it interesting that Helen would have hung onto the letter for so many years. John chuckled as he rose from his seat to leave. She wanted to make sure she had the last word, even if decades later.

John drove to Charlotte Motor Speedway. There was no race this day, and the track sat empty. He decided to read Helen's letter and wanted privacy. He could do that much, since she was terminal. John did not carry animosity toward Helen; he had moved on and did not want to relive the past. He was resolved not to see her and could not care less what Michael thought of him. There was no relationship between them to damage or to lose.

John sat in one of the luxury suites overlooking the track and pulled the letter from his pocket. The paper was soft from much handling. He recognized Helen's loopy and neat writing style and began to read.

First let me say, I have loved you very much, have always loved you even before you realized it. Making a life with you has made me very happy. My fear of your racing was my fear of losing you. During the past several months, I have come to realize that your racing IS you—that

*my fear has caused a deadening of any affection you
have for me. You need me to encourage your racing, to
encourage you. I suppose I finally heard you. The fact that
you have cared what I think about your passion, that
you wanted me to understand who you really are, shows
there was some affection and concern on your part. Why
should I let my fear impede your life? I have to confess,
John, I also have resented the pursuit of your dream
when I have felt uncertain of what my own should be.*

*So, I decided to surprise you by attending the
race in Abbottstown—to support you by being
there with Michael and Susan. Today was
to have been a fresh start full of hope.*

*As the race began, a strange feeling came over me and
I wanted only to leave. At first, I thought it was fear
of the race and pictured your car in an accident. It
was fear, but not of the loudness of the engines or the
possibility that something bad might happen during the
race. It went much deeper. It was a foreboding sense
that a shift was taking place—a change in who you
are—that everything had led gradually to this moment
and a switch would be flipped that would irrevocably
impact your life and mine, as if you were going someplace
where I would not see you again. The feeling was only
momentary, and I was able to relax and watch the race.*

*I watched your car every moment. Your skill is amazing,
John. I met a couple in the stands who told me how you're
the up-and-coming star of NASCAR and felt so proud.*

*When I saw you cause an accident, it seemed I
was watching someone else. It is so unlike you to
intentionally hurt someone to get what you want—so
different—but I've never experienced a race and
reasoned that perhaps hitting other cars to get them out
of the way is normal. Yet I wondered ... would you
hurt me if I stood in your way? Today, you have.*

*Seeing you with your woman friend, the two of you
together, we have never had that kind of interaction
that oneness. I understand now that you never
have loved me. Not real love that yearns to spend
a lifetime of shared experiences. Perhaps that is
why I never saw you pulling away from me, John,
because you were never close to begin with.*

*We never will have a deep love without much time and
committed effort, neither of which I believe you will be
willing to invest. If I am wrong, tell me. If you do love me
enough to dedicate your heart to me as your wife, to start
over as I have decided to do, we can move on. Otherwise,
I have decided to let you go. The choice is yours to make.*

John folded the pages and stared out onto the empty
track, now splashed with gold from the sinking sun, and
realized that Helen knew him better than anyone did. She
too had sensed the change that had set in at that race—that
had been gradually encroaching on him for years. How
would things be different, he pondered, if he had read the
letter so many years before? Despite the excitement and ego
stroking that Maggie provided, he did love Helen then and

was stunned and embarrassed when she abruptly told him the marriage was over. He had left immediately, showing up on Maggie's doorstep. John had gone back home a few days later to collect the rest of his things. Helen assumed he had read the letter and had made his choice. She had been cold, accusing him of ruining a man's life so he could get ahead. She had been more accusatory and negative than ever. She wanted out, she said, before his ambition ruined him. By then the papers were full of the accident, printing pictures of the blazing Chrysler and black smoke pouring into the sky. The driver of the car John had rammed would never drive again; the accident left him a paraplegic. John reasoned her accusation away. Racing could be dangerous, that was the risk, what made it exhilarating. Drivers bumped other cars all the time; it was his job to win. It wasn't his fault the other driver couldn't control his car.

"It wasn't my fault." John confirmed his thoughts aloud.

Helen's words that night had been correct: racing was everything. His relationships were validated only by how they correlated to his pursuit. He thought of Max "Pop" Vogt, of his long-time crew manager, Mark Underwood, and even of Maggie. Each one played a role in his success. What was wrong with that? No, he reasoned, there were leaders and followers. He was a leader. Actually, he was fine with that.

Chapter Nineteen

Thaddeus

I'VE NEVER SEEN THE nurses in such a tizzy, running from room to room, barging into bathrooms, opening closet doors, practically peeking under the beds. They've even got me searching the place, as if I had nothing better to do.

The head nurse is giving me a hard time, "Thaddeus, where is he?" she's almost hollering at me. "You must have taken him somewhere. He's not capable of getting out of bed himself."

"Why would I do that? You think that's my idea of a good time, hiding patients on you? He must have wandered off."

"Impossible. It's just not possible."

Well, I don't know about that, but Mr. Powers was looking close to the other side when I left last night. He wasn't even calling out like he normally does. Now they can't find him. It should be interesting when his son shows up tomorrow—I can't wait to hear the explanation. Think I'll come in early just to witness it. Now they have the doc involved.

"Have you checked the morgue?" The head nurse says and flashes me one of her looks.

The nurse tech is coming to my rescue. "He was lying in bed comatose a half hour ago," she says. "Thaddeus insists he has not moved him, nor has anyone else on the floor."

The doc has been listening to all this with no expression on his face; just listening, and now he is telling the head nurse what to do. "Put out a code yellow. If he doesn't turn up in half an hour, call the police."

John cautiously opened his eyes to the onslaught of another day. Fuzzy, gray walls morphed to white as his eyes gradually focused. He lay in bed, slowing gaining consciousness, waiting for the pain to register. There was no sound and there were no voices; no footsteps hovered outside his door. They must have moved him during the night—he didn't recall the window looking quite like that.

Now fully awake, a strange mix of panic and delight rushed through him as the realization hit: there was no pain! No stabbing pain in his gut, no dull weight on his chest or ache permeating his bones. He could feel no tubes down his throat or needles in his arm. He lifted his arm and gasped. Smooth and taught flesh, strong veins, tanned skin with dark hair. He must be dead. That was it. He had died in his sleep.

John powers shot out of bed and stared at his surroundings. He saw a bedroom simply furnished, a dresser topped with female paraphernalia—cleanly organized. This room felt familiar. A wind-up alarm clock on the dresser told him it was just past eight. John felt energized, light. If he was dead, why did he still have a body?

He ventured out into the hallway, blinking to see if the vision would vanish, slamming his body back into its true present state. The short hallway seemed almost cozy. A plush rug stretched warm and soft under his bare feet. This was not a cold, hard hospital corridor. Photos hung on the walls. He investigated one and found a fresh portrait of Michael and Susan as he had known them so many years ago, aged three and one. A maple-stained wood door led to a small bathroom where a mirror hung over the sink. John approached slowly, his heart pounding, afraid of what he might see. The mirror beckoned. John's jaw dropped as his image, all of twenty-one, stared back and then broke into a smile.

A faint, muffled voice carried into the room and drew John back into the hallway. It was coming from downstairs. Helen. It was Helen's voice. She sounded so young! All at once, John knew where he was. This was their first house in Pittsburgh, bought just before Susan was born. He followed Helen's voice down the wooden steps and into the brightness of a morning kitchen dancing with color and sunlight. Helen sat next to Susan's high chair, coaxing a spoonful of scrambled eggs into her mouth. Michael sat adjacent, working on a bowl of cereal. Three sets of eyes met his.

John stood, bewildered and overcome with the sight of his youthful family.

"Where are your clothes, Daddy?" Michael laughed. John shot a glance down, relieved to see a pair of boxers in place.

Helen stood and approached, wrapping her arms around John and planting a quick kiss on his cheek. He recalled what a beautiful, happy girl she had been. She always wanted to do the right thing, was always taking care of her family. He had not noticed then. "Good morning. Would you like some eggs?"

John's body tingled from her touch. How long it had been since anyone had touched him, really touched him, in a caring way. Maggie had been gone over ten years. He could not remember. He could not find his voice to respond.

"Is anything wrong?"

"No! No, I'm fine. Sure, some eggs."

Susan pounded her chubby hands on the high-chair tray.

"You go get dressed while I finish up here. Then we can have breakfast together before you leave."

"Leave?"

Helen looked confused. "For the race. Isn't today your race in Abbottstown?"

A reminder about race day sounded strange coming from Helen. She never kept track of when or where his races occurred. John ran his hands through his hair and held his head as if trying to will memories to the surface. "What's the date?"

"It's Friday. May 25."

It had to be 1956. The NASCAR Grand National ran there in '56. He had won the race that day. What was going on? Why was he here? John's mind ticked back to recall the events of the original date. Abbottstown.

"Are you coming?" he asked Helen.

Helen looked surprised. *"Nnnno.* Why would I come? You know I never attend races. Besides, it's three hours away, and with the kids …"

"Fine, I was just asking." At least things were true to form in this strange place John found himself. Would anything change? Maybe Helen would not show up at the track, would not see Maggie. By whatever providence allowed this day, John did not care. He only knew that he felt exuberant. John Powers would yet again zip around a dirt track to take first place.

Pulsing with energy and anticipation, he took his young, strong body upstairs to find something to wear. This must be heaven; where else could it be? He was preparing for a race he knew he would win.

The smell of petroleum and metal oozing from the rumbling Chevy made John high. He was so keyed up, he feared he would jump the start and be disqualified. A swell of expectancy coursed through him as he waited for the green flag. Could he still run a dirt track, any track, with the skill and agility he had then? Could he keep it up for two hundred laps?

His apprehension vanished at the flash of green overhead. The Chevy cruised along the track, tight and responsive to John's every move. He marveled at the simplicity of the car compared with the latest models he had favored. It was beautiful, intense, thrilling. He hoped he would be able to stay in this place at least through the race to experience the fullness of it.

As easily as breathing, John slipped into the zone, the Chevy an extension of himself, of his thoughts. He rode within inches of the other cars, strategizing and finessing, working every turn. Getting in front of third eluded him. That Chrysler sitting in second was strong, the best contender he had ever faced. It seemed the driver could read his mind, knew when he would ride up the track or attempt to pass, and moved into position to prevent it.

All right, there was still plenty of race left. He swapped fourth position twice and moved back a few spots after a pit stop. By lap 150, he was back to kissing the Chrysler's bumper, trying to outsmart and outperform its driver. "Come on, buddy, this is getting old."

Approaching lap twenty, John knew he would have to do something soon to get out of third. He took the inside track at the fourth curve, gunning the Chevy out of the turn. He advanced, but not enough to get alongside his opponent. His right fender sat behind the Chrysler's left taillight. He knew the Chrysler would move back down to block him once more. If only he could get around him!

Time amplified. A pack of thoughts charged through John's mind in the flash typically occupied by only one. The setup was perfect; John would bump him out of the way and scoot past on the inside track. He slowed ever so slightly, creating some room between the two cars for the bump to be effective. They were on the straight and the pack was getting tight. He had to move now!

His leg muscles tensed, preparing to gun the Chevy into the left six inches of Chrysler tail end that he could reach.

Then his mind mercifully remembered the groan of metal as the Chrysler flipped and landed at the fence. He recalled fire, smoke, paralysis, accusation.

Instantly, John eased off the gas, crying out with the frustration of lost opportunity. Turns one and then two were upon him. Another lap, the fourth turn, loomed. The Dodge in first made the curve and held a groove near the inside track. Attempting to gain ground on the Dodge, the white Chrysler stayed at the outside track and bore down. It was enough. John slipped ahead and rode rim to rim on the inside grove. The pair rode astride for several more laps until finally, with only five to go, John had gained enough track to push the Chrysler up at the second curve, slipping down in front. Now the Chrysler was looking at the white backside of John's Chevy, holding squarely in place. He could feel the glare penetrating the back of his head. Due to the roar of his engine, he could not hear the crowd burst into wild cheers as he grabbed second.

The Chrysler was past history. Now he had to chase the Dodge running in first place. It would be a good show for the spectators, John thought, a close call to the end when he would slip ahead to take the lead. Only three laps to go. The Dodge held the inside track and refused to let go. John managed to pull the Chevy alongside the Dodge's outside fender but lost momentum at the turns. At the last straight, John mashed the pedal to the floor. The Chevy gained a few inches on the Dodge, almost door to door now, as the pair raged over the finish line.

Second. John was stumped, but he let it go as he finished the lap and pulled up near victory lane to watch Buck Baker take the prize. Other than his choice not to ram the Chrysler into oblivion, what was different? Had the commotion of so many years before caused the Dodge to slow enough for John to catch up and pass? Perhaps he was a more aggressive driver then. Whatever the reason for not taking first, John Powers was thrilled to be on the track again. Second was a good place to be on this day. The crowd spilled from the stands and onto the fringe then surrounded the winner. What else, John wondered, would be altered? He waited. Fans were approaching now, eager to witness this handsome young man accept his winnings. John smiled. He posed with his colorful Chevy and shook the hand of race officials.

A reporter approached. "John, I'm from the *Pittsburgh Post-Gazette*. We're writing a local interest piece. What can you say about your success as one of the youngest member of NASCAR?"

John barely had time to form an answer. The crowd pressed closer, their voices drowning out his thoughts. John felt confused. Something was not right, was missing. What was it? He tried to concentrate, to remember. The sensation of what was historical reality and present reality blended and melded in his mind until, tired of struggling with it, he gave up. A calm sensation washed over him and the conviction and peace that whatever happened now was meant to be. For this moment, he did not have to be in control.

"John! John." A woman's voice called from the swell of people that had wrapped around the Chevy. There! It came again. He searched the faces and then he saw her. Forcing her way to his side, a youngster in each arm, was Helen. John's heart leapt to his throat and hot tears sprang to his eyes. The emotion fought for escape as he struggled to manage the feeling of love and support that washed over him. He had experienced the same sensation before when spotting his parents, Pop, and Susan proudly waving from the stands after his first race. He had placed second on that day, as well. Second place felt incredible. Second place still did.

He reached to take Michael from Helen's arms, to draw her and Susan beside him. "These are with me," he proudly stated.

He lifted Michael up and perched him on his shoulder. Helen stood close at his side, pressing next to him. John noticed that they had dressed for the occasion. The *Gazette* reporter's camera snapped away, and soon others followed.

"Hey, Powers," a voice called out, "is that the next NASCAR grand champion?"

A swell of pleasant laughter emanated from the crowd.

"No," John said, "he's going to be a lawyer." More laughter.

Helen gave John a questioning look, raised an eyebrow, and shrugged. Holding Susan on her hip, she held tightly to John's arm with her other hand. She was shaking. John realized how much courage Helen needed to be there.

John fielded more questions until the crowd began to dissipate.

"Powerhouse."

John turned to see Maggie, stunning in her blue brocade, slowly approaching from the retreating crowd. He gave her a faint smile. *Here it comes,* he thought. *Confrontation.*

She approached the little family. John lowered Michael to the ground, holding his hand. "I just wanted to say congratulations and to comment on what a beautiful family you have."

"Thank you."

Helen smiled pleasantly, yet John could sense that she felt uneasy. Apparently, Maggie sensed it also.

"Forgive me for being so rude." Maggie extended her hand to Helen. "I'm Maggie Saunders. My husband and I have been customers at Pop's Garage for, oh, since this guy was in high school."

Helen's voice revealed her relief. "Oh! Yes, hello, Maggie. I'm Helen."

John stared into Maggie's eyes, trying to read her thoughts. Was she still married? Had that changed as well? The ring was missing, but it would not be the first time she had removed it. John determined that she was not. Why else would she drive over three hours to see a race alone, dressed in her statement piece, if not to spend time?

"That was quite a performance today, Mr. Powers," Maggie continued. "You have ambition. I like that, and with such a wonderful family to support you …" She looked straight in John's eyes, ensuring that he captured every word. "That is everything, John. Hold onto it."

"Yes." He returned her gaze, hoping to convey how much she had meant to him, how influential her support had been. She smiled through sad eyes and hurriedly disappeared into the waning crowd.

John knew what Maggie was doing. She was letting him go.

Chapter Twenty

MICHAEL STRODE ALONG THE corridor toward room 210. A handsome man in his fifties, he held a confident gait. That in itself was enough to warrant stares from the hospital staff, who seemed vaguely intimidated by his presence. He sighed to find the room unoccupied. He didn't have time for this; he had somewhere to be within a half hour. He took the guest chair and waited, flipping through a dated copy of *Newsweek*.

A familiar voice sounded from the hallway. "Thaddeus, can't you make this thing go any faster?"

"Well, I'm sorry, Mr. Powers, but all that's fueling this baby is me."

"Humph. Well, that explains a lot."

The pair entered the room. John, dressed and ready to leave, sat in a wheelchair propelled by Thaddeus.

"Son! You made it. Get me out of here. They have nothing that goes over two miles an hour."

"That's your problem," Thaddeus said, "going too fast, racing at your age, and on dirt. Amazing they still do that. It's a wonder that crash didn't break every bone in your body."

"It was for charity and I only broke two bones." John patted the cast on his leg and winked at his son.

"We'll be sorry to see you go, Mr. Powers." Turning to Michael, Thaddeus said, "He has told us many fascinating stories about his early racing days, about NASCAR, and we understand you are quite the accomplished attorney."

"Thaddeus," Michael broke in, "can I have a word before we leave?"

"Sure. You hang tight, Mr. Powers. We'll be back momentarily."

Thaddeus followed Michael into the hallway and down the corridor, where they were out of earshot.

"Look," Michael began, "I've got some people waiting so we need to cut this short. Can you meet me downstairs in the next ten minutes?"

"Sure, sure." Thaddeus's voice deflated. Michael handed him a slip of folded paper and disappeared down the hall.

"Where's Michael?" John asked.

"Says he's going to meet us downstairs. He's in a hurry."

"Oh." John became silent.

Thaddeus wheeled John, wordless, down one corridor, then another, to the waiting elevator. Reaching the first floor, he bypassed the lobby and made a right.

"Uh, Thaddeus, I think you made a wrong turn. The way out is back there."

"I know where I'm going."

"But …"

"I'm just following instructions."

They wheeled past the cafeteria, the gift shop, and the chapel and came to a glass-paneled door leading to a large courtyard heavily landscaped with trees and flowering plants. The door slid open to birdsong and the scent of warm earth. Confusion washed over John as Thaddeus followed the narrow pathway that was now curving around a clump of bushes. Perhaps this was a different way to the parking lot where Michael would be waiting. He was in a hurry.

"Surprise!"

John jumped in his seat and then broke into laughter. There, amid dozens of colorful balloons, stood Helen, Michael, Susan, their spouses, and two generations of grandchildren among a host of friends.

"You missed the post-race party," Helen explained, "so we thought we'd bring it to you."

The youngest Powers baby, John's infant granddaughter, was plopped in John's lap, and he was at once swarmed by hugs. Michael stood protectively behind John's wheelchair, rested his hand on his father's shoulder, and gave a strong squeeze. The reassuring male gesture brought Pop to mind, and for a moment John felt surrounded by the good will of everyone he knew, had ever known.

Just as suddenly, John sensed a deep aloneness, gray and still, creeping into his soul like a dream reminiscent of another life. The sensation lingered momentarily before heaving its last breath and dissipating to nothingness. John felt stunned and more than a little shaken.

"Michael, are you there?"

Michael stepped around and kneeled down to face his father. "Do you need something?"

"No." John looked down at his hands, dark and thick veined. "Yes." He rested a hand on Michael's shoulder. "I love you, son."

Michael laughed softly. "I love you too, Dad. You know that."

John smiled. Victory lane had never felt so good.

There are times when being a hospital tech has its advantages. Take now, for example. I can't remember the last time someone shoved a piece of cake my way and insisted I enjoy myself. Well, so be it. Don't know what's better: the cake or watching these nice people lovin' on their papa. I've seen people come out of a coma with less fanfare. Strange, but nice.

Actually, things have been strange all around lately. Just the other night, I had that dream again, only this time it started off worse. Here I was, wheeling a corpse down the hallway like before, but this time I was sobbing and hollering something awful. Felt like I was coming apart. Did I wake up? No, kept right on dreaming, all the way down to the end of the hallway.

That's when the dream changed. The door swung open and, instead of the morgue, I was heading outside. The gurney had turned into a wheelchair and my patient, he was sitting up and ready to go. The chair stuck a moment at the door, as if the brake was on, but I gave a shove and we wheeled into the warm sunshine. When that happened, I felt real good, like when a problem that's been eating at you is finally solved and you can move on.

That's when I woke up. Almost hated to do it ... I wanted to see what happened to my man. Guess I should have kept sleeping all those other times. Who would have thought it would turn out the way it did?